Hell Found Me

By

T. O. Jacks

Contents

Hell Found Me

I could pretend to be saddened by it, or surprised, but why bother with pretence? Sighing deeply, I released the tension, anxiety, and yes—I could now admit it—the fear that I had been carrying for these past weeks. Bringing the double-shot glass to my lips, I swallowed deeply. For the first time in weeks I could feel tequila's smooth burn as it slid across my tongue and down my throat—the difference from one sip to the next, bile to libation.

Hell found me. The acceptance of it allowed me to relax. I could let go.

Lifetimes on the run come once again to a brief pause. Hell's voice was less a sound than a feeling, not heard but felt: a brief reprise from games.

Laughter escaped my tequila-loosened lips before I could pause to ponder the repercussions. But then Hell had found me. What was there to lose?

"I'm having another drink," I said, waving the young bartender over. "What does Hell prefer to drink?"

Ever the sinner, always content as long as your needs, no, your wants are satisfied. The voice of Hell had the feel of insects crawling along my skin. Bloody Mary Hell told the bartender.

I was comfortable enough with my fate to accept it, but I could not look it in the eyes. I instead looked at the bartender's expression when he responded to the voice. What did he see and feel when Hell spoke to him?

"Sure thing." The young man smiled.

The hand that rested lightly but deathly cold on my shoulder had alerted me to Hell's arrival. Now it slid across my back. Its cold deadened my skin, freezing everything it touched. It killed my body hundreds or thousands, if not millions of cells at a time on its path to a resting place at the base of my neck. Feeling Hell's amusement by its actions chilled my body even more.

Is this a game? If it is a game, is it over? If this is a game then maybe, just maybe I could win, I told myself, forcing myself to focus on Hell's amusement by torture. Trying to ignore the sound of my own body's dying cries, this is a game I could win I repeated to myself

It was a game. Hell's voice transformed from the feel of insects walking along skin, to the feel on mosquitoes buzzing around ears. You had no chance to win.

Looking back in time, I knew I'd had several chances but life had always stood in the way, either living it or surviving it.

Many people say that there is always a choice. That is true. There is always a choice. You can live, you can die, or you can survive. Sometimes, but not often I'd had the chance to live those moments I gobbled up like a child long-denied sweets. Most often though, I'd had to fight to survive. And on occasion, less rarely than I'd prefer, I'd had to use all my strength not to die.

Reflection, at this late date? Hell's laughter was ice on the skin—but not the slow, seductive movement of a single cube along sensitive skin on a summer day. Hell's laughter was dry ice held directly to skin for agonizingly extended moments.

No. This was a simple answer that may not have been entirely true. Not reflecting … self justifying. Was that sound my voice or that of a petulant child?

There is no justification. The hand moved from the base of my neck to trace along my spine; the voice again crawled along my skin, no longer insects, but now thousands of pinpricks, burning cold. The law is absolute, cut and dried. You can walk in the light or you can live in the darkness. There is nothing else.

Stating that fact pleased Hell in a way that slowly killing my body did not. Turning those words over in my mind gave me pause. Walk in the light or live in the darkness. How sad it would have been to me if this were the beginning and not the end.

But this is the beginning a mosquito buzzed at my ear. It is always the beginning; just as a thing is constantly ending, it is at that same time constantly beginning.

Just as everything ends something new is constantly beginning. Is that true? I wondered.

No! Burning cold hit me in a searing jolt beneath Hell's deadly cold annoyance. There is nothing new. Not you, life, the choices you've made or the choices you could have made. This thing you now call life has been lived time and again. Every road has been taken, every choice made and time and again Hell finds you, here. Annoyance had become cold satisfaction in the telling that Hell always finds me.

My glass had been refilled but just as before, Hell found **No table of contents entries found.**me. Upon bringing it to my lips, instead of sipping tequila, I swallowed bile.

"No matter what choices I make….." I could not contain the sob that choked the words in my throat. "No matter if I walk in the light … Hell finds me? That could not be true."

It is not true. Truth is a subjective, mortal thing. Truth dies with the teller. This is a fact undying, no matter who sees or tells it. Time and again Hell finds you. Always Hell finds you, here.

"If I walk in the light?"

The brightest light casts the darkest shadows. When you walk in the sunlight do you not see them?

"Yes but—"

Take heart. The hand now fell on my thigh, slowly, seductively killing me. You will do this time and again for eternity.

Knowing that I was caught in an endless cycle of choices that could not save me, gave me the lack of emotion needed to look at the face that had come to take my life.

Hell cannot take your life. Life cannot be taken.

The face I saw held beauty so pure that my eyes burned to see it. I knew that I was blinding myself looking at it but I could not turn away.

"You are beauty." I sighed, knowing that I had been gifted with a view of true beauty in its purest form, beauty beyond human comprehension. I now gazed at the beauty of an angel. The light beneath its skin burned the sight from my eyes. I gladly accepted the darkness caused by that light.

Energy is neither lost nor destroyed. It is simply transferred from one body to another. Do you understand?

I could not comprehend the words that the insects crawling along my skin spoke to me. My mind was busy fighting to retain the memory of beauty for which sight had been sacrificed.

Hell Found Me

Sadness unlike any I had ever imagined existed closed over me in the darkness of my mind as the memory of beauty quickly faded. I now mourned—not the loss of sight but the loss of the image of beauty.

Beauty is fleeting, dry ice laughing along my skin rejoiced in telling me, as is flesh. The cold hand lay lightly on my chest, over my heart, freezing, killing, enjoying the death of warmth. But these things you know.

"Hey." The young bartender had known to keep his distance from that one. But after a long while he knew that it was time to say something. "Hey, you okay?" A light tap on the shoulder caused the body to fall in a way that no body that held life would fall.

I was totally released from the Hell that moments before had been the body that I feared losing, the body that moments before I thought losing meant death, I followed in the darkness to my place in eternity. I could feel, more than hear, the young bartender panic. I would have found humor in it if not for the insanity of it. How do you laugh along the road with Hell, along a road in Hell?

I wish I could remember while still wearing flesh, all the many times alone in bars, saloons, taverns and ale houses having that last drink as Hell found me.

Insanity

Evan watched as the blood beaded red on the tip of the long knife that he held dripped into the growing puddle on the floor and wondered if he would get away with it. The old man was a fool and had died a fool's death. Moving to the open window, Evan breathed deeply as the night washed over him. A cool breeze free of the smell and taste of blood soothed him.

"I am finally free of him and I will be able to live my life now. I am not a murderer; I am a saint. He tried to make me into a tool of the evil one," Evan justified.

"But the old man was always there for you—the old man never lied to you." The voice that often spoke in Evan's mind chided him. "You have done a very bad thing. You will be punished for this and there is nothing that can redeem you for taking the life of one that meant you no ill."

"But he…"

"There is no excuse for what you have done this day," the voice said.

Evan protested. "But Gerald told me…"

"Why offer excuses when you feel no remorse?"

Evan did not understand why the voice would treat him this way after being silent for so long. Why would the voice now tell him that he had done something so terrible but when Evan was considering this action, the voice stayed silent. Could Evan now not even trust himself? Evan was sure that the voice was a part of him. Why would Evan betray himself?

Insanity

"Why are you turning against me now?" Evan asked the voice, his rational mind accepting the fact that he was having an internal conversation with himself. "Why would you, if you were so against what I have done, not counsel me against such a horrible action? You are also at fault. You are to blame for the death of one so innocent, if there is such a thing, which I seriously doubt."

"You are the fool and you will die the death of an ignorant blind fool." Evan now imagined that the voice spoke from behind him.

Closing his eyes to lean his head against the window Evan sighed. "You are one to speak of fools. You are the fool for even holding this conversation with me at a time when it is irrelevant. Why wait until the life has been taken? It cannot be returned. Why wait until the blood is spilled and cooling? You are a hypocrite and I would prefer that you no longer bother me with this foolishness."

"Do you not care that you will be punished? Do you not care that you were used? Do you not understand what has happened?" Evan could hear the voice moving behind. It sounded as if the voice paced back and forth in agitation.

Turning, Evan faced the small man behind him and spoke aloud slowly. "It is you who have betrayed me. It is you that should be punished. It is you that has waited until there was an act committed that could not with all of my power be taken back, to speak in the name of what fools call reason. Why now, I again ask? Why? What is there to gain by letting me do this while you sit idly by and watch, to then condemn me to punishment?"

"I called to you but you would not listen. I tried to help you but you would not accept it. Gerald was in

9

your heart and you chose to pretend that I did not exist. I am not strong enough to stand against you in your own mind. You chose the way of the evil one in listening to someone that would lead you in the way of power and material things."

Evan turned away from the imaginary man behind him and the voice in his mind that insistently told him he had committed an atrocious crime. Evan again closed his eyes and deeply inhaled the night air. Evan always felt powerful when the light of the moon shone on him. It was as if the dark of night was an energy that he could absorb through his skin and the light of the moon was the beacon that told him where that power should be directed.

"You, as well as I, will be punished for this crime—you for committing it and I for allowing you to do this thing," the voice told him. "You have ruined the both of us and you are too stupid to know it is unfair that I should have been bound to you in this way. It is unfair and I am now to suffer for your mistake. I should dispose of you now."

"You cannot dispose of me, you fool. How dare you even suggest such a thing? Are you even more foolish than you pretend that I am?" Evan sighed, shaking his head.

"I could punish you myself for your crime and then maybe…"

"Maybe what, you idiot," Evan asked, irritated. This conversation with the voice had taken what Evan considered a ludicrous turn. How could Evan be talking of punishing himself to avoid punishment? Maybe the old man was mistaken in his thinking that Evan was a saint and that the pressures of Evan's power and duty to the world were driving him to the brink of insanity.

10

Hell Found Me

Maybe Evan was already insane and that was why he had killed the old man.

"That is what I will do. I will punish you and then I will not be so severely tortured for what you have done" the voice reasoned to itself.

Evan, who had been lost in his conscious thoughts, looked behind him at the small man walking on the table who was now lost in thought. Evan could see that some sort of conclusion was being reached, but he could not make himself focus on the man. Evan knew that the voice was his mind's manifestations of his own inner thoughts and self. Evan also knew he had a duty to perform and would finish this discussion with himself at a later date.

Looking at the blood that had pooled and would congeal if given time, Evan focused on the white-hot power within him, the power that was fueled by the life that surrounds everyone, but was very rarely if ever noticed by most people. Feeling his center warm, Evan pulled this power from his abdomen to his chest and then to his hand.

The white light that came from Evan's hand in a powerful, blinding burst, wiped the room clean, removing evidence of his crime from the carpet and floor. The power Evan used converted the matter to energy, as flame does burning wood. But in this, the most pure of energy conversions, there were no ashes or traces of what once was. The person who once existed on this earth and grew from boy to man was now the wind that would propel a ship. The old man was now the rain that would water the earth. No longer was he something as fragile as a man or as finite as a human being. The old man was now a part of life.

"I have given him a gift." Evan said aloud to the voice. "I have made him more."

"You have broken the law." The voice said now on his right shoulder. "I will have to punish you. You are a saint. It is not your place to interfere with the lives of mortals. It is not your place to take or to give life. It was not your place to give him the gift of becoming a part of the circle. I have to punish you."

A tentative knock on the door put an end to the conversation that Evan was ready to end with himself. The fact that Evan was talking to himself about punishing himself in such a way, made Evan think that he may actually do himself harm. It was puzzling, and on a deep level, disturbing.

"Yes?" Evan answered the knock.

A small woman entered the room and looked around. She did not seem surprised to see that there was only one person in the room.

"The old doctor usually takes his tea now. It helps him sleep." she said softly. She did not look into the eyes of the man who had been coming for many years to see her old master. There was something about her that the old one told Evan he would never understand. "I thought that he was in the room with you, but I do not see him here. Is there something that I can do for you while I wait for him?"

"There is nothing that you can do for me. And there is no need to wait for the old one," Evan said. "The old man will not return. He's gone on to another stage of existence."

The woman finally looked at Evan. Something in her expression gave Evan the impression that she did not understand what he had just told her. Evan was sure that

12

her gentle nature would shield her from readily comprehending such things. She was timid and fragile.

"So then my old master is dead," she stated simply, standing a little straighter. "You say that the old one is no longer of this plane of existence?"

"He is not," Evan stated simply.

"His body has been committed to the abyss?" she asked, looking at Evan for the first time directly in the eyes.

Evan did not answer. The woman had been a servant in the house of the old man for as long as he could remember. This was the first time that Evan ever saw her stand straight. This was the first time that her eyes were not downcast. This was the first time that she looked as though she was not merely a slave but a person. Evan had done a good thing in releasing her from the prison that the old doctor had kept her in. She had been a slave and now she was free.

"Have you disposed of the body, Saint?" The change in her voice was now more apparent as Evan relaxed with his back against the window.

"Why are you asking me this?" Evan asked, not alarmed by the sudden changes. Evan was sure that she had been fighting for her freedom for years and now that she was suddenly free she should wonder what happened. Evan would not, of course tell her the whole story, but he would let her know that she was free of her tormentor.

"She is dangerous. I had not noticed it before, but now I do" the voice cried desperately inside Evan's head. "You must destroy this creature now before it is too late. That is why the old one kept it so close and so subdued. She is a danger."

Hell Found Me

"I will not kill an innocent. She was a slave and now she is free. What right does anyone have to take the life of another, or to keep another in servitude? You chastised me for the taking of the life of the old doctor and now you tell me to take the life of one that cannot protect herself" Evan hissed indignantly in his mind. "To take the life of one that has been used as a slave for the many years that I have come here. Why would I? Why would you suggest such a thing? In asking me, you are asking yourself to commit such a crime."

"Where is the body?" the woman asked, boldly taking a step forward. "I need to see the body, or has it been completely destroyed?"

"You are free of the old man. He is no more." Evan told her turning to face the window so that he could inhale the night air, to take energy, power from it. In Evan's mind he could see the green that was the life-force of the elderly man whom he had helped release his ghost. Evan would use the strength of the old one to rebuild his own. "He is no longer here to keep you oppressed."

"Ah, Saint," she said, licking her lips and looking towards Evan's right hand that still held the long forgotten knife that had taken the life of the old one. "There was a thing to which I was bound. As time passed and it grew weak, I was able to flex my power and feel my freedom just a beat away. This thing to which I was bound must be destroyed completely for me to be free. As I cast out with my mind and I search, I cannot find it. My power seems to come back to me. It is as if I were long asleep but it was an unnatural sleep, as if I have for years been drugged and now I am awake. Power flows through me as currents in the ocean. I must know where the body is? Has it been completely destroyed?"

14

'The body…"

"Tell this demon nothing, for she will surely kill you, and then she will go on a rampage. This is a true problem. Kill her if you can, and if not, bind her." The voice coming from Evan's shoulder near his ear was desperate now. Please undo this wrong that you have done. She searches for his heart. She will eat it if she can find it. But because we know not what type of bind the old one put on her we will not know what needs to be done to break it, though I am sure that the ending of his life will have set her for the most part, free. "How has he had a demon here in this house and I have seen her so often and not known it."

"You are still young," she said, looking directly over Evan's shoulder at the full-sized man that crouched on the windowsill. "This is the first time you were assigned to guard a saint. You have spent all of your time in the kingdom. I have seen you on several nights when your young saint had fallen asleep and you spoke to the old doctor." Smiling with crimson eyes ablaze, the large, slightly feminine form stepped forward.

"What are you talking about?" Evan looked at the man in the window and then at the form approaching. Evan was now sure that he had lost his mind. Was this his punishment for taking the life of another? The man on the ledge was a figment of his imagination, a face that he had created to accompany his inner vice. There were times that the things which the voice told him were odd, but Evan had always been sure that it was manifestations of his subconscious imagination at work.

"We will not let you leave this place. There is no way that the work which the old doctor has done will be forfeit," The man said, placing a hand lightly on Evan's

Hell Found Me

shoulder. Evan shuddered at the weight and warmth of the hand that rested lightly on his shoulder. "The saint I guard may not be as strong as some but he is powerful and I am sure that you cannot defeat the two of us."

"Don't be a fool, my brother. He is of no use to you now," the demonic voice said mockingly. The sound had become that of insects on flesh. "He is still in shock to find that you are not a part of him but his guardian." The voice mocked when it added, "And seeing as how you were with him, guarding him, how is it that he was allowed to kill, to take the life of one so pure of heart without your intervention?"

"I'm going insane" Evan cried inside. "I've lost the slight hold I had on sanity."

"I will destroy you before I am judged," the man said, standing in front of Evan more solid than Evan had ever seen him. The man was tall, standing well above Evan. His features were striking in a way that no movie actor's could be. Evan's imaginary man was more real than anything Evan had seen in his life and at this moment more real than Evan himself.

With that sight of the man in his defense, Evan finally found clarity. Evan was the one at fault and Evan would be the one that would correct his mistake. Evan would bind the demon and Evan would take whatever punishment that his guardian administered. No one should suffer for his foolishness for the first time in his life Evan knew; it was his mistake and his responsibility.

"No, Jonathon. I have done this thing, my friend. I will make right what I have torn asunder." Evan placed a hand on the solid shoulder before him. It was warm, comforting to touch. "I, a saint, have murdered a binder in cold blood. It is of no fault of yours. I will bind this demon. And I shall banish it as well."

16

"But Evan—" Jonathon protested.

"No. I see now what for these past years I did not, and I thank you my friend." Evan smiled at the man in front of him then turned to the demon facing them. "How many" Evan asked the towering form in front of him. Mocking laughter was his answer.

"Tell me how many and you will receive the mercy of a painless end," Evan said softly. He inhaled the essence of the old man, feeling the old doctor's power, friendship, and wisdom. "How many were bound to the old one?"

"Like you have the power to bind or banish," Gerald said stepping into the room. "You could not even hear the cries of protest from your guardian for the last three weeks. You are a fool and you are weak. You lust for the life of a human and in that lust you have ignored the rules by which you are to live. You have sacrificed your soul as well as the freedom of your guardian and worst—or is that best?—you have set me free."

"I will not let you free of this place." The guardian was now holding a sword that shone like the light of the moon. "You were foolish to try to escape in this way. You knew that I would do anything.... I would risk all to prevent it. You cannot stand before me. I cannot be killed, and by you I cannot be defeated." Taking a step forward, the guardian raised his sword.

"No!" Evan cried out. "That is not the way with these. And we need to know how many. We could defeat these two and there may be others that we let escape."

"Because you are so much our friend," the deformed body of the female laughed, "I will answer honestly."

"There is no other. I am the only one." Gerald finished.

"So there are only the two of you?" Evan smiled taking a step forward. "Good."

"No. There is only the one." The guardian told him. "This is a disaster. We cannot defeat him. The old one was very powerful indeed if he was given the honorable task of guarding it. This is Fiend. We are doomed."

"And now that I have been so honest with you in the number of demons that were here, I now ask you one question. Where is the body of the old one? Where is his heart?"

"It is no more" Evan answered in despair.

"Good." They smiled. "Then we are free."

Jonathon (funny how now Evan knew the name of his guardian) rushed forward to try to prevent the two from touching, but though his speed was such that Evan was sure no human could follow his movements, Jonathon could not keep the two halves from becoming a whole.

The sword flashed as Jonathon tried to cut the two as fingertips touched and then solid became liquid and the connected mass began to bubble and reform.

Jonathon, standing midway between the two when they touched, was touched by the bubbling reforming mass. Alabaster skin instantly began to blacken, as purity of heart was soiled by malicious intent and ill will.

Evan watched as if there were a grotesque play unfolding before him. The two halves still separate but fast becoming one, reached down and took his friend into their hands.

"Jonathon will no longer exist if there is nothing done," the old man said inside Evan's head. "You must say the words and feel the life within your heart as you say them."

"As long as my flesh knows life, as long as I am a part of the cycle of energy and power, as long as my heart is true...." Evan heard the words and knew they issued from his lips; the voice was not his. "As long as my spirit is conscious, as long as there are two, I bind you. You cannot escape my justice. You will always feel my wrath. My power is a shield that keeps you from destroying my future as well as reliving the past. I am your master. Bend to my will as air is supple, yet powerful still. Two from one, corruption gone forever, slaves until time is gone. The day I am no longer is the day you will be free but bound for time eternal. You are in servitude to me."

Two naked forms lay beside each other on the floor—one female, one male. Jonathon lay between them, insubstantial but breathing. The moon sword was gone from sight.

"How have you done this old man?" cried Gerald, the name of the male half. "You are no longer alive, I am sure the saint killed you."

"He took the life of the mortal body that was beginning to fail me but he also granted me a gift." The voice of the old man spoke from Evans lips. "He used his power to turn me to life energy. I am now a continuous part of the cycle of life No more do I have the failings of a mortal body." The old one laughed. "Your murderous plan has backfired; now that I am nothing more than life energy you will never be free, because I cannot be killed. I now have no heart to destroy. You have damned one saint, but you have guaranteed your imprisonment for eternity."

19

Hell Found Me

The look of rage and hatred that was directed at Evan warmed his skin. Evan would have turned away if he had any control of his body, but he did not. Evan also could not overlook the fact that the old man had mentioned him and the fact that he would be damned.

I will be damned? Evan thought sadly.

For all eternity, the old one answered. You have committed the crime of murder. Though in the end you saw the error of your ways and it was more of a benefit to the kingdom than to those who would use you, the laws are absolute. Your guardian will be punished as well, though he cried out to you and got no answer. This is the path that you have chosen to walk. This is the payment that you will receive.

There was a time that Evan would have railed against this cruel fate. There was a time when Evan would have thought it unfair, would have said that he was tricked into doing something that he would not have done had he known, and it would have been true. Had Evan known the consequences of his actions Evan would never have done these things. In the past Evan would have cried foul because he would not want to suffer. But Evan could now see that as long as life was lived only in fear of what ill would come to him, then there would be no growth. Evan only existed before. He was now ready to live.

"I don't want Jonathon to suffer for my folly. I want to take responsibility for my actions. I was gifted with free will and I used it to make the wrong decisions, to make mistakes to live. Why should others suffer for me?"

"It is not fair!" Evan's heart cried out for Jonathon's injustice.

Insanity

As Jonathon walked the dark street he smiled to himself. The lesson had been learned. The young one, Evan, was in the dark, torture chambers where he would stay for lifetimes reliving the pain of self-realization over and over again. Evan would continue to live the night he murdered his father until he no longer thought that his punishment was unfair, in any part. The night before Jonathon was released when Evan admitted that he had used his own free will in making the choice to take a life. How long would it be before the young man accepted the law and bended to it?

"I hope it will be soon," Jonathon said, shuddering.

The fact that the young one had played the most vital of parts in binding the Fiend for eternity was the reason that the Master did not send him to the pit. The fact that the young one would not accept that in taking the life of the old one he had broken the law, and the laws were absolute for the good of all. This was the reason the two had spent centuries being punished for arrogance. The guardian always suffered with his charge.

"Please, Evan. Learn from this and come back," Jonathon said, looking to the moon. The insanity of life could always be seen in the moon.

An Enforcer's Bond

After what felt like a lifetime of waiting he was assigned *the mission*. The wait ended with the call to meet privately with Specialist Commandant Ford the Chairman of the Joint Chiefs of Staff and the President of the United States. The small part of him not numb from waiting was awed and impressed. Three of the most influential men in the world had personally assigned him this mission. The honor would have been humbling if he had not known they felt his death was the inevitable end to this assignment.

The men who assigned him the mission weren't aware he had been following the progress of this situation over the past eighteen months watching the twelve Specialists before Ambrose that were assigned this mission die as he waited patiently to prove himself, hungry for his chance. When Ambrose returned more dead than alive he momentarily mourned the missed opportunity. Everyone before had Ambrose died Ambrose however returned in honor, but he later learned not victory. The mission was not completed. He knew that after Ambrose's defeat he was next in line for the opportunity to give his life just as he knew that where so many others had failed he Jade would succeed.

Everyone assigned this mission before it finally made its way to Jade was a delegation grey demolition class specialist physically the most powerful people in the world or thought to be until Jade enrolled at the compound academy. The twins told Jade that compound faculty tried to keep Jade away from this mission because he was too young. They didn't want this to be his first mission. The compound did not want to lose its star before it had the chance to rise.

Jade was the first ever to fit the criteria to become a delegation red, enforcer class specialist. When Jade entered the academy there was talk that he was the only living being powerful enough to fit the criteria.

Jade was a shape shifter but not lycanthropic. He could withstand more physical damage than most Demolitionists and heal himself. Jade's natural defenses mental as well as physical were stronger than anyone at the National or International Security Specialist Compounds had ever seen in one person. With his body's natural resistance to damage and pain as well as mental shielding Jade was considered the total package strong both physically and mentally where most were weak in one or the other.

Coming toward the end of the long flight that would take him into the situation area Jade decided to land for a moment and rest. The terrain was flat and barren and from the air Jade saw no sign life for tens of miles in any direction. There was no concern of being seen or taken unaware.

Jade was currently in his primal form having decided at the onset of this mission that it was the best camouflage. Any human who saw Jade would think he was an eagle, an exceptional eagle, but an eagle none the less. The zoologists at the compound had done extensive research on Jade's primal form the first months after his arrival and classed him originally as a Red Eagle but later he was re-classed as a Red Tailed Hawk. Jade's dorm mates, the twins, had laughed for a long while at the irony of that discovery. Most people that saw Jade's primal form automatically thought he was an eagle due to his size which was for the best in most instances as eagles were a protected species of raptor where hawks sometimes were not. The few overzealous hunters that were unfortunate enough to think Jade's primal form a prize for the taking had gotten personal instruction in the use of talons on human flesh. Jade had been trained by the best to defend himself by any means necessary and had no qualms about it.

For a moment Jade pondered the morality of his situation. Was it wrong, Jade wondered, and should it be considered murder as opposed to self defense to kill someone you know cannot defend themselves against you, someone that you know is weaker slower dumber, even if they are trying to cause you harm? As his first assignment this mission meant a lot to Jade he saw it as an opportunity to jumpstart his career having been granted an opportunity most Specialists straight out of the academy would never get. Thinking once again to the morality of killing a defenseless human even if they didn't know that they were in essence defenseless against him. Jade sighed, there was no way he would let an unsuspecting human poacher ruin his chance to prove himself. He would complete this mission and at the age of twenty-three Jade would be recognized as the power everyone speculated him to have the potential to become. Jade would come home to praise and honor he would come home in triumph and ask Amber to marry him.

Amber, the thought of her made Jade shudder. Amber was the most beautiful gentle woman Jade had ever seen. Jade's friends teased that Amber would never get rid of him, raptors mated for life. Amber and Jade had been dating since five months after they met. The exact amount of time it had taken Jade to convince

Amber that she wanted him desperately and not the other way around. They met shortly after she began her training at the compound.

It sometime surprised Jade that such a gentle woman could hold power over him. Jade Hawk, first Enforcer in history and hopefully after this mission the National Security Specialist for the state of Michigan knew to be careful with what he said and did around his girlfriend of the past two years ten months twelve days. Standing a staggering 5'3" tall at 117 pounds with smooth golden skin and eyes without raising her voice or using violence Amber ruled Jade's world… with an iron fist Jade had to admit, but he liked it. Amber's brown hair was baby soft and always smelled like jasmine it felt like silk on his fingers Jade reminisced. As soon as he got home, after showering of course, Jade would ask Amber to marry him.

The mission Jade thought shaking himself he had to concentrate on the mission or Amber would be mourning and moving on.

To draw his thoughts away from the sweet comforts of home Jade decided to go over the details of the mission, knowing it would keep his mind from straying. Jade knew that what some might consider useless information could turn out to be the tidbit that saved your life, the difference between returning healthy and returning less one limb. Though this mission was one that would make the hair on anyone's head stand on end.

At a midpoint location somewhere between Sidi el Hadj ed Dine and Benoud in el Bayadh Algeria a terrorist group had formed and was expanding. They felt that things in the world needed to be changed and that they were the ones to do it the usual terrorist thyme, but this time their leader Morhat Da N'yet found a secret weapon, a lycanthrope, more specifically Morhat discovered a werewolf.

Morhat trying to find a secluded place to set up his base of operations chose a place in the desert outside of what he thought were abandoned ruins. According to compound intelligence this took place at the same time the local werewolf pack began to experience internal strife, the local pack that claimed as their territory and safe haven the dilapidated buildings the terrorists decided to neighbor. Compound intelligence felt it was sheer dumb luck the budding terrorist group did not decide to take residence inside the buildings. Though the terrorist camp was only about fifty miles away from the land the pack called safe haven they were not hunted. The local wolves had their own worries at the time.

Months after the terrorists settled in the local pack held a fight for dominance during which pack leader Ackhbar Penoit was defeated. Before Penoit could be killed by Daniel, no last name provided, Penoit's mate interfered, saving his life and giving him the chance to flee. Penoit left his mate to the mercy of the pack when injuries suffered interfering in the fight slowed their progress.

Because of his injuries Penoit could not travel far so he fled to the area the terrorist camp occupied taking refuge on the outskirts of the camp. Penoit was aware that the members of his former pack avoided the solders and the area their camp occupied. Penoit sure he would not be openly hunted near the camp settled in to rest until he was healed and had regained his strength.

After the fight for dominance and Penoit taking refuge in the shadow of the terrorist camp Jade felt that the story of the terrorist camp got a little fuzzy. It was

26

said that shortly after taking residence Penoit was captured by a patrol from the camp but escaped. The terrorists not knowing what they captured did not understand that better facilities would be needed to hold Penoit than iron chains and a tent in the middle of the camp. Penoit began to hunt the terrorists and soon the once thriving facility of close to five-hundred had dwindled to a mere three-hundred fifty or so, or so information gathered said.

Eventually Morhat captured the leader of this one-man attack on his camp and cause, alpha male and former leader of the local wolf pack Ackhbar Penoit. While transporting the prisoner Morhat noticed Ackhbar's strength and the smooth efficiency with which he moved setting off warning bells deep inside Morhat. Looking into the strange eyes of the man now captured and soon to die Morhat saw no fear he saw only patience and anticipation as if to be taken into the camp would be a treat for him.

According to Specialist Ambrose's report Morhat often spoke to his men of his early experience with Penoit saying that Penoit's eyes were frightening they were so much like those of an animal. Morhat set up a tent outside camp so that he would not have to bring Penoit into his base camp. Morhat questioned Penoit personally and when Morhat finally learned Penoit's secret Morhat realized that he had at long last found the means to change the world. Morhat would finally be powerful enough to do the things he envisioned.

To pacify Ackhbar and to gain his trust Morhat allowed Ackhbar to hunt some of the men in the camp. The men given to the werewolf were those Morhat thought would not be able to accept his new vision, those not strong enough to follow his new plan for

Hell Found Me

world dominance. Weeding out the weak reduced Morhat's numbers greatly the camp that was once 500 strong was by the end of Penoit's fun close to than half its original number.

After a sufficient amount of time Morhat asked Ackhbar the question that would change the face of terrorism in the world for years to come, or so Morhat thought. Morhat Da N'yet convinced Ackhbar Penoit to infect him with the lycanthropy virus. The promised return favor was the annihilation of his former pack.

After Morhat was infected the rest of his plan fell directly into place. There was a three-month transition period during which Penoit taught Morhat to control the beast within when the transition time was complete the bargain was to be upheld. But of course when the transition time passed the terrorist Morhat betrayed Penoit and killed him. Taking Penoit out with a group of solders for the supposed extermination of Penoit's former pack Morhat had his men surround Penoit shooting him repeatedly, when the injured former pack leader lay wounded and defenseless Morhat cut off his head and had his men burn the body.

With the murder of the former pack leader out f the way and the body disposed of Morhat began to methodically change his people. Slowly the terrorist group gained power and recondition all over the world unfortunately for Penoit's former pack they were not forgotten. Morhat went back and hunted and killed the local wolf pack using the destruction of the local pack as a test of the strength and assimilation into the life of lycanthropy of his men many of whom died disposing of the local pack sheer overwhelming numbers being the only reason the local pack was defeated by the newly turned terrorists.

Jade's mission was a simple one. Find and destroy the remaining lycanthropic terrorists and bring their leader justice… no sweat Jade thought. When the mission was first assigned it was given to a lycanthrope, the thinking being that lycanthropes born were more powerful than those infected as the terrorists encounter with the small local pack had proven. The compound sent several men to their deaths and seriously injured another before they decided to try a different tactic. Jade often wondered why a group was never sent in… why this was an assignment that was repeatedly given to only one person at a time as if someone at the compound wanted some of the most powerful Specialists killed.

When the sun set Jade took flight locating natural caves as he surveyed the land making note of three locations that could be used as daytime resting places. After choosing one and dropping off his large pack Jade set out for the camp his intention to observe the activity and awareness levels of the camp. At approximately 1:45 am the campsite came into view. According to reports from satellite observation there were approximately seventy-five terrorists on the base at the start of Ambrose's campaign. Specialist Ambrose confirmed making eight kills on his visit and wounding at least seven.

Jade circled the camp for about forty five minutes, watching the guards and the scant activity taking place on the nearly deserted base before coming to a landing spot fifty miles downwind.

Once on the ground Jade's mind began to race if an alarm went up and all sixty seven of the remaining lycanthropes converged on him Jade's death would be a long painful concert of torn flesh and agonized screams. Whatever attack he implemented the key would be stealth though Jade was more than a match for any five lycanthropes the sheer numbers in the camp could overwhelm him as they had his predecessors not to mention the deceased pack that once inhabited the area. The fact that the terrorists were lycanthropes that had military training was even more of deterrence to rushing in. These things taken into consideration Jade also had to shake off the thought of killing them one at a time by luring them away from the camp or any others that could raise an alarm. Killing them individually would be slow and after a short time the camp would go on alert and begin to hunt him.

Jade was positive Morhat would expect and was awaiting this next attack. Why would the world governments give up after sending so many? The destruction of this camp was a necessity to world security, but how would he do it? Jade couldn't rush in and attack and he couldn't kill them one by one. Taking to the sky Jade began to again circle the camp watching their security formations and activity levels monitoring the five guards on duty. The guard pattern around the camp formed a loose pentagon shaped perimeter.

On impulse Jade swooped down and grabbed one of the guards. One talon lodged in the guard's back instantly breaking his spine as the other crushed his skull. Jade flew back to his downwind drop spot and ripped the head from the body before returning to circle over the camp.

There was more activity in the camp but not much the only indication that the guard's disappearance was noticed was the eight men standing in the spot the guard was taken from. The men were speaking to each other and gesturing into the night. Some of them stopped to scent the air but none of them looked up.

No one ever looks up, Jade laughed to himself. Grateful for his luck, Jade thanked god that the blood from the dead guard did not seem to have left a useable trail, or seemed to be noticeable on him at the time.

Jade flexed his mind and formed one human arm, his right. As he circled above the camp Jade stretched to loosen up the muscles in his arm that were stiff from the repetitive motion of flying. No one seemed to understand that when Jade formed wings and arms at the same time his arms and wings were not as strong as they would be if he only used one at a time, the muscle and bone were shared, Jade's body mass did not change it shifted which was why Jade was much heavier than any person or bird his size would ever be. Jade's overly dense skeletal system lacked the hollow honey comb structure that made avian bodies lightweight and flight easier. Avian skeletons were light which is why Jade could not fly until he turned 13 he simply was not strong enough to carry his body that weighed close to five times what a human child his size would.

Shaking off memories of childhood insecurities Jade reached over his shoulder and wings to unsheathe the silver sword strapped to his back. Circling high overhead Jade saw that the group of eight had become ten all of whom were standing in a close circle still talking, Jade imagined they were discussing the missing guard feeling this was as good a time as any to start his attacks Jade tightened his circles over the camp building speed with his spiral decent. With his sword held out as he passed dropping rapidly to shoulder height Jade severed all ten heads on one tight circular round. Velocity in addition to the sharpness of the sword made the decapitations relatively easy. The difference in the men's height a non issue none of them were short or tall enough to save their life.

When Jade regained the sky over the camp he noticed that there were nine other people in view in the camp. The four remaining guards and Jade assumed their replacements as well as one lone wanderer. Jade decapitated them all silently his feet not once touching the ground. Jade had not left his scent on anything but the air, and that was washed clean by the desert breeze. No alarm had risen.

Jade noticed the smell of morning on the air and decided to retreat for the day. To the northeast there was a sheltered cave about four hours flight from the camp, found before the nights exploits began.

Jade calculated as he flew, one plus ten plus four plus five plus the last one, twenty-one of the remaining sixty-seven terrorists that Ambrose left alive, that only left forty-six to kill. Jade knew the coming night's kills would be harder. The bodies would force them to be on alert. One guard missing was one thing but twenty severed heads was quite another. The lack of tracks might give them the notion to look up, though that was not the natural inclination. Jade was going to have to plan well for the upcoming night's raid though he knew that it might be prudent to wait a night or two to continue his attacks on the terrorist camp with the evidence of his first night's activities making his work difficult Jade steeled his resolve to attack again at full dark.

Releasing his primal form Jade stretched his 6'8" form from head to toe and removed his weapons and pack pulling on a tattered pair of shorts. Making his way to the rear of the cave Jade cleaned and sharpened his sword before going to sleep.

Hell Found Me

When Jade woke he ate a small amount of dried rations took a nutrition pill and dug his bow out of his gear. The arrows were all silver heads with silver worked into the forty-eight-inch long shafts. Once outside the cave Jade took on the form of a bird with two human arms. With bow and quivers across one shoulder sword across the other Jade flew out to the camp again. The desert nights were extremely dark and from his position above the people in the camp would not be able to see anything but darkness on the chance that they did look up Jade on the other hand could see them clearly.

As Jade approached the camp he noticed the changes before he got close and could not help laughing. The camp was well lit and the guards were paired off. The bright light made it even harder to see anything in the air but all ground activity was easily seen from above.

Jade pulled two arrows from his back knocking one to the bow as he flew the other he held in his beak. Poised and ready Jade waited for an opportunity. Jade's roommates at the compound said it looked just plain weird when he donned arms in his primal form, but it was comfortable making an excellent marksman better. The sight of a hawk is much better than that of a human, even one with 20/5 vision. Jade could focus on the most miniscule of objects tens of hundreds of feet away like a hawk sighting prey from the sky above. Jade focused on a guard's right eye and came down to within range of his bow just beyond the lights of the camp. The release of the first arrow nock and release of the second was so fast that the second arrow was released within seconds of the first. The second guard fell as an arrow pierced his heart through his back and came through his chest before he had the time to turn to his fallen comrade. Jade had two more arrows ready as another

33

guard came to investigate the small sound and the smell of blood. This guard took an arrow through his right eye. Jade gained altitude and circled the camp killing the other eight guards in much the same way. Jade then began to monitor the camp to see if anyone would venture out into the seemingly deserted camp.

During the course of the night Jade came down to decapitate three men, one making his way to the bathroom, and to Jade's surprise he caught a couple out on a tryst. The lovers found on the southwest corner of the camp behind a Hummer died quickly Jade landed on the back of the dominant thrusting his sword through both their hearts pinning them together for one moment then decapitating them to be sure they were dead.

Jade circled the camp for a few more hours and when the new guards came to take the place of their dead counterparts he killed them. All but three died with arrows through the eye or heart. The guards coming in sets of two died before they reached their posts. The only problem was when the second shot on one of the guards went wide and Jade had to come down and using a talon rip the head of the guard from his body, the noise raised an alarm and Jade had to fly up and out of sight quickly. No more covert kills could be made that night.

Jade was so pleased with the night's success that he did not stop to think about the fact that decapitated bodies had been left lying in the middle of the camp for hours and the smell of blood had not alerted others in the camp. The alarm should have risen not from the sound of surprise made by the missed guard, but the smell of blood from the dead guards' bodies.

Jade flew back to his hideaway camp and counted his second night's kills as he cleaned his sword. Twenty-four kills that night Jade tallied with a smile as he settled in for sleep. The first night had left forty-six terrorists alive and twenty-four kills this second night left only twenty-two terrorists to kill, no, twenty-one because their leader was to be brought back alive. Morhat was to be brought back to the states to the compound for his execution.

Thoughts of the night's hunt made Jade's body warm with pleasure. Jade would take out the guards whittle their numbers down to about ten or so and then he would land in the middle of the camp and kill the remaining few as they came face to face as men. Jade would bring the fugitive Morhat to justice and then he would ask Amber to marry him. Jade went to sleep thinking how good it would be to go home. Amber would be glad to see him home safe, and he would just be happy to see her. Jade fell asleep in his primal form.

The moment Jade woke he knew something was wrong. The dim light that barely made it to the back of the cave told him it couldn't be past 5:45 am maybe 6:00.

Why did he wake? Jade listened to the faint rustling sound outside the cave. Someone was trying to sneak up on him. Jade adjusted himself over his sword, still in primal form. The bag with his unstrung bow and arrows was behind him against the wall.

"I'm telling you I saw it go in here." A male voice whispered from outside the cave. "It hunts at night. That's why you've never seen it. "

"Shhh, you fool!" Another male voice "If this bird's as big as you say we just want to shoot it and bring it out of there" The sound of a gun safety being released.

"No, you fool! " A female voice chided. "Use the tranquilizer or you'll ruin the feathers. If the bird is as big as you claim it'll be worth more alive, or at the very least with the body undamaged."

Poachers, Jade laughed to himself using his beak
Jade plucked one of the feathers from his back ignoring
the brief intense sting of its removal. Jade then changed
to man form, quietly slipping on his tattered shorts.

"What was that?" the woman hissed.

The woman must have heard something but
after realizing they were poachers Jade was not worried.
Jade picked up his sword and said "who is there?"

"There's someone in there you fool." The
woman whispered then said to Jade, "Sorry sir we
thought you were a bird."

"There is a bird why don't you come in and see?"
Jade laughed to himself knowing that he was inviting
trouble but could not resist, justifying his actions with
the thought that these people, at least one of them, had
been monitoring him and would need to be disposed of
before Jade could safely bring his prisoner back to camp
for transportation back to the compound for trial.

Jade speared the feather into a clod of dirt and
tossed it to the mouth of the cave. If they were poachers,
as he knew they were, the size and color of the feather
would bring them into the cave to kill the poor soul that
was guarding such a valuable prize. Jade would kill them
and go back to sleep no problem.

"What was that?" The second man said jumpily.
"Why is there blood?"

"I'm telling you there's a giant hawk in there."
The first man spoke again adamant about what he had
seen… that one would definitely have to die.

"Come in my friend" Jade said changing his feet
so that hawks talons extended from his toes gripping the
dirt in anticipation "come in and see."

The sound of laugher outside the cave, bestial laughter, gave Jade pause had Morhat and his people followed him back here…

"Yes my friend I do think it is time we see you" a growling voice said.

Jade dropped his sword and grabbed his bow and arrows. Damn! Cursing himself for being arrogant and talking instead of remaining quiet Jade strung his bow and notched an arrow in record time. An arrow between the eyes of the first humpbacked beast made the others pause.

Lycanthropes, Jade could see now from the body of the first to darken the mouth of his cave, just as the bestial laugh had told him.

"Move him!" The female voice said.

Jade's aim, accurate as only a bird's sight could make it, shot through the skulls of the two lycanthropes that tried to remove the body from the mouth of the cave.

"Daniel!" The female screamed, "You will die interloper! For what you've done you will die!"

How many more Jade wondered. He'd only had thirteen arrows when he returned to the cave that morning and now he only had ten.

"I'll come out" Jade shouted as he put down his bow and picked up his sword. "Please don't hurt me… I'll bring you the bird…I just…" Jade feigned nervousness and was sure that his anxiety could be taken as base survival fear. Jade focused on his feet to fully form his talons holding in his groan as his two center toes on each foot merged and his little toes relocated to the back of his feet to point in the opposite direction. The lycanthropes just outside the cave would smell Jade's primal and human forms in the cave and Jade was

Hell Found Me

sure that they would think that there were two beings in the back of the cave at least for a moment. Jade knew that they would think of him as prey and prize, but he wanted to come out of the cave and not knowing how many there were outside made pretending weakness and fear the best plan at the moment.

Rotating his wrists Jade briefly considered staying in the cave it was a defendable position, but for how long against an unknown number he was unsure, they could wait him out or work him in shifts until he was to tired defend himself or they could simply overwhelm him in the cave and block his escape. Taking a deep breath as his talon feet gripped the earth beneath them Jade threw his body into motion speeding through the cave jumping over the three bodies at the mouth of the cave forming wings as he did so Jade ignored the pain of his partial transformation allowing the muscles in his arms to atrophy for a moment Jade pulled most of his muscle tissue into his wings so that he could swiftly pull himself into the air with powerful strokes of his wings.

Once in the air circling his hideaway and taking account of his attackers jade evenly dispersed the muscle between his arms and wings. From the air Jade saw that there were only five more of the lycanthropic poachers, plus the female. They stood outside the cave in a semicircle looking up at him in awe of the 6'8"man with giant wings.

As Jade started his decent three of the lycanthropes scattered at the sight of his approach. The two others stood transfixed as if the sight of their impending death hypnotized them into stillness. The severing of the passive onlooker's heads as he passed them, Jade was sure, sufficiently broke the spell. Jade landed beside one of the three that ran startling the man

Jade used a two handed grip to chop the burly body in half. Jade turned to see one of the others changing direction trying to get away from impending death. Taking his sword by the tip Jade hurled it piercing the fleeing Man's heart through his back. Surveying the area Jade noticed that the female was missing, as was the last of the males.

A shot rang out piercing the silence of death. The bullet caught Jade in the upper left arm pushing Jade to once again take to the air. The last man stood atop the hill above the mouth of the cave shooting at Jade with trembling hands. On his assent Jade snatched the gun from the man's hand shooting him in each eye Jade thanked his lucky stars for trembling hands on his enemies.

Jade flew a circuit of the camp but there was no sign of the woman. Landing Jade decapitated the body not killed by his silver arrows or sword as a precaution then went to the mouth of the cave still seeing no sign of the woman Jade knew she must be inside.

The pain in his arm made Jade disgustingly angry he would have to take time to heal and that meant one more night away from home. After Jade healed himself he would need rest not to mention the lack of today's sleep. Jade couldn't kill twenty-two lycanthropes wounded or exhausted.

"Come out now!" Jade called irritation lacing his voice. "For your own sake don't make me come in there and get you."

There was a soft rustling sound in the cave and then the female came into view, weeping and dirty. Jade looked at the woman closely she was small, maybe as small as Amber and scrawny. Looking closely at her Jade realized she was pretty, and if she were fed she would be voluptuous and beautiful. Her black hair was matted and her skin had a sickly yellow cast. There were dark circles under her eyes that made her large eyes seem sunken into her face.

"I'm not afraid of you bird" she said defiantly her voice was strong and clear, if everything else abut her was pitiful.

"For your own heath, don't make me any angrier than I already am." Jade said shaking his head as he let his wings melt into his back feeling some of the strength return to his arms and then turned to retrieve his sword.

When Jade turned back to his surprise the girl had not run, or tried to attack him, maybe that was for the best. After looking at her Jade had decided to let her live, but he wanted to keep her with him until his mission was over. It would be stupid to let her leak word of his presence to anyone.

"You belong to a pack near here?" Jade asked wondering if she was a member of what was left of the local pack or if she and her friends were the result of bodies left behind that were not quite dead. Jade needed to know the status of the area. Eight of them had come for him he needed to know how many more there were, how far away and how long before they would be missed.

"Is there a pack close to here?" Jade asked noting the defiant look in her eyes Jade sighed and turned away, damn hungry scared women, that was all he needed right now.

Jade retrieved his arrows from the men's bodies he had to leave the area immediately the smell of blood was making it a hot spot. After removing the arrows from the men's bodies Jade walked to the woman and slapped her to her knees.

Hell Found Me

"Answer me now or die, slowly, how many more" Jade said in what he hoped she thought was a menacing voice. Using the point of a silver arrow Jade scratched a jagged line down her arm. She looked up at him with hungry tear filled eyes, but did not answer.

"Fucking women" Jade muttered to himself.

Jade did not have the stomach to kill her if it were not necessary she was small and hungry. She may have been stronger than a human woman her size, but starvation screamed at him not much stronger. Jade grabbed her arm and pulled her to the back of the cave where he bypassed his coils of silver rope and tied her up with nylon string. Jade then gathered his supplies, removed any trace of his presence from the cave, and forming wings on his back picked up the woman and flew away.

Before his first attack on the terrorist camp Jade found two back up caves Jade relocated to the secondary refuge fifty miles to the southeast. It was a smaller cave but more easily defended Jade had chosen the larger cave for comfort, feeling that he could easily defend himself.

Sitting the female inside the cave Jade loosened the rope enough for her to feed herself and gave her one of his food rations. Jade sat facing her and dug the bullet out of his arm laughing when he looked at it. Silver, they had used silver on him as hungry as they were they used money for silver bullets.

To bad for them I am not a lycanthrope Jade thought. It didn't matter what they shot him with. If they were not fortunate enough to pierce a vital organ and kill Jade instantly he would heal.

Jade gathered energy to heal focusing inside knitting muscle and skin together reforming shattered bone. Repairing his arm took Jade just under fifteen minutes. There was no scar but using that amount of energy left Jade starving and exhausted.

Snatching up the supply bag Jade consumed a day's worth of rations and water. Glancing to the side Jade noticed that the woman had eaten and fallen asleep. The desert night was cold and she was trembling. Jade pulled a Thinsulate blanket from his bag to cover her then changing to full hawk form Jade settled in close to the woman and went to sleep.

Jade woke to the sound of the female calling him softly.

"Bird, Bird please wake," she whispered. "The solders are coming, Bird please," She sounded terrified.

"I'm awake," Jade muttered.

She had squirmed behind him in the cave Jade could feel her trembling with fear.

"Stay quiet and don't move" Jade said in a calm voice as he moved from the cave and flew out to see what was happening.

Circling high above the ground Jade saw an uncovered Hummer fifteen miles northwest of his cave. Jade could easily see the passengers and after getting a closer look Jade saw that Morhat was among them.

The sight of the terrorist leader in this vulnerable position made Jade forget how tired his body was. The possibly of being able to complete the mission and go home was all Jade thought of as he flew back to the small cave. When he got to the cave Jade paid no attention to the frightened woman huddling in the back as he retrieved his bow and arrows and flew back to the Hummer. Jade laughed at the fact that they had the top off exposing themselves to attach from above.

The two guards died within seconds of each other. Morhat tried to run but Jade swooped down and

Hell Found Me

grabbed the terrorist leader none too gently talons piercing flesh Jade felt the muscles in Morhat's shoulder tare. Returning to the cave Jade tied Morhat from head to toe with the silver rope and gagged him then staking the terrorist to the ground. Sword in hand Jade then flew to the terrorist camp. The thought of Morhat trying to escape the camp in the night gave Jade the impression that the job could be finished easily.

They were afraid Jade could taste their fear from the air above as he approached. The fact that there were only three guards on duty made Jade drunk on the prospect of killing indiscriminately.

Jade pulled into position over one of the guards then holding his sword tip down in a two handed grip Jade folded his wings he fell towards the ground. Jade's sword entered the guard's head at the crown and did not stop its downward motion until it was firmly lodged in the ground. Jade stood pulling his sword from the ground and let his wings melt into his back feeling the muscle in his arms become denser and more powerful Jade smiled with wicked excitement. Turning towards the center of the camp Jade felt none of the fatigue from earlier that day, there was no hunger... for food.

As Jade walked through the camp he held his bloody sword in the air to attract the other guards to him. The few guards that were brave enough challenge him approached slowly not attacking him until a small group had formed. All Jade could think as he cut a bloody swath through them was the sheer animal joy part of him felt at killing. For a moment Jade's primal form threatened to overcome him so that his beak could tare into flesh and he could taste the fresh blood that he spilled.

Hell Found Me

What a waste Jade's primal core thought as he walked away from the fresh kills not having consumed any of the fresh meat.

Jade's circuit of the camp took him lastly to the large central tent. As Jade opened the flap and walked in he realized why Morhat had fled. If they had not caught up to Specialist Ambrose when they did, Jade would not have gotten this assignment. The central tent was where all the injured were kept. Jade realized why the smell of blood had not caused an alarm to raise. Those found in this tent could not defend themselves they were so badly maimed that the underlying smell of blood had long since become a part of the camp. Jade much like humans could not smell the blood as acutely as lycanthropes could. It had become a way of life for the people in the camp they could not distinguish the smell of the camp from the smell of the freshly killed guards. The murder of those in the tent was so easy Jade could not even make sport of it he merely went from bed to bed and loped off a head.

When Jade returned to his small camp he ate fed the woman then went into a coma like sleep finally succumbing to the drain of healing himself and immediately attacking the camp.

Two days later when Jade felt rested enough to start the trip home Jade turned to the woman and gave her all the arrowheads he had gone back and retrieved from his victims leavening no trace of the camp was part of the job. Upon waking from his initial deep sleep Jade went back to retrieve all his arrows wipe the place clean of himself, and of course, torch the place.

"These are of value." Jade told her "Silver, you can sell them for food there are no more lycanthropes in the area unless there are more that you are not telling me about. But I promise you that all of the solders are dead."

Turning away from the woman Jade changed to full hawk form not bothering to remove his tattered shorts as there was now a hole in the back for his tail Jade took his prisoner in talon and pulled into the air. Jade glanced at the woman standing there looking up at him as he flew away. *What is she thinking* Jade wondered briefly then put his mind to the task of getting home.

The flight home took five nights with many stops along the way. When Jade reached the compound he went immediately to the administrative offices and Commandant Ford's office door.

Jade dropped his prisoner like a bag in front of the door and released his primal form just as the office door opened.

"Jade" Commandant Ford said "Good to see you". He looked down at the man on the floor in front of his door. "The assignment doesn't seem to have been too difficult for you, come in let's talk."

As they entered the office Ford called for someone to come collect the prisoner.

When Morhat was taken officially into custody and things settled down Commandant Ford said "What I am about to tell you is off the record of course, but you will be named the Security Specialist for the state of Michigan tomorrow morning. It is the greatest honor that can be bestowed on a field specialist to be the specialist for the state where the compound is located where all Specialists come to train Do you want to know why someone so young would be given this honor?' Ford asked looking Jade intently in the eye.

"Because I have just done what a dozen seasoned specialists could not." Jade answered.

Hell Found Me

"No Jade… at least not entirely" Commandant Ford said shaking his head. "You will get this position because of your delegation and class. You are the first and for now the only Specialist ranked as Enforcer. That means part of your job is to regulate the specialists."

"Sir" Jade was stunned.

"You know how specialists are classed don't you Jade?" Ford asked.

"Yes "Jade answered reciting first year lessons, "Specialists are tested for their physical and mental abilities including defenses and offensive weapons capabilities gauging how powerful they are and in what area."

"Well to a point you are correct. They are tested for power but there are also psychiatric tests that are administered to see what type of personality they have what their mental state is just as the F.B.I. or any other law enforcement would. You can't let a mental case have authority over the general populace. The reason you will have this particular position is because you are one of the most morally correct people to come through these doors. Not to say that you are a choir boy but in most instances you will do the morally right thing."

Jade was stunned

"Close your mouth boy." Ford said. "Don't act so surprised. Do you think that just because these people are more powerful than others that they're good people, that they'll do the right thing? God no, hell Jade some of them fit the psychiatric profile of kidnappers rapists and murderers. Most of the Suppliers, if not all are cold-blooded killers with a few ugly twists on the side that's why the Enforcer Delegation was invented in the first place. We just never had any one person who could fill it. Until now Specialist regulation was the job of a group

46

of administrative officers of the compound. There was never any one active specialist to do it. To be honest there was no one powerful enough to do it, and then you came. The twins could do it even though they are not as physically powerful as you are… not that that matters as powerful as they are… but they feel that they are not properly suited for the classification of Enforcer. Not to mention they have scared a lot of people the enforcement they've done…it's been… chilling." Jade watched Commandant Ford shiver the twins were Jade's closest friends and had been his roommates from the moment the three of them entered the compound and even still they shared on base housing. "But I digress, the point is with all these people federally licensed to kill and trained by the best to do it efficiently and without a trace someone has to have the job of monitoring them. Think about it Jade, you must know that someone has to 'police the police' shall we say."

Jade thought about it for a while then asked "If I kill a specialist?"

"You'll have a shit-load of paper work ask the twins. But its part of the job you know." Ford told Jade "Now don't you kill people just because you don't like them. You will be held accountable if there is no justification for the termination and we'll have to send the twins after you. But I don't think you'll have any problems. I recommended you for this job personally."

Jade nodded and then asked "Sir I've noticed that Amber is going into her last term next year and she has not been classed yet. Could you tell me why?"

"You know why" Ford said giving Jade a knowing look.

"Sir, if you don't mind I have to be going." Jade said noticing the clock the mention of Amber's name reminding him that he hadn't seen her in so long.

"Amber waiting" Ford smiled

"Yes" Jade answered. Jade was wearing a pair of ragged denim cut offs that could withstand his transformation and he smelled as if he had never had a bath in his life but patting his pocket the lump of the ring box made Jade feel calm and sure.

Ford noticed the movement and asked what was in Jade's pocket. Jade smiled as he pulled the box out.

"This is the ring I'm going to give Amber when I ask her to marry me today… after a shower… as soon as I see her I'm going to ask her."

Ford looked at the ring and nodded it was a small diamond that would look nice on Ambers delicate hand.

"Why don't you wait until you look at your assignment bonus before you ask her?" Ford said pulling an envelope from his pocket "Amber is a very pretty girl 90% of the men on the compound are going to hate you for taking her more out of reach than you already have but I knew the first time I saw the two of you together." Looking past the clock on his desk Ford said "You had better be going Amber is on her way here now."

"Thank you sir" Jade said as he stuffed the envelope in his pocket and left the room.

Jade closed Commandant Ford's door and walked to the stairwell. Just as he was about to take the first step Amber's voice stopped him.

"Jade Marcus Hawk stop right where you are." That voice stopped him instantly Amber had used his full name. "How long have you been home?" her voice was quivering when she asked. Jade turned to see her

Hell Found Me

soft full lips set in a pout. Amber's golden eyes were full of tears.

"What's wrong Amber" Jade asked confused thinking she would have been at the very least happy to see him alive after so long a time apart. Something had to be wrong.

"I was so worried." Amber said sighing as she walked to him and laid her head on his chest. "To see you're home and haven't even come to see me or sent word to me that you're ok" Amber stepped back and punched Jade in the stomach then looked down at his clothes. "Why are you naked?" She asked running her finger along the upper rim of his ragged shorts, making Jade's stomach quiver "What have you been doing?"

Jade was tired, and the barrage of questions coupled with her touch had robbed him of his ability to think clearly let alone answer any of her questions.

"Jade!" Amber snapped stomping her foot to get Jade's attention.

"Amber," Jade said taking her shoulders into his hands." I just got back to the compound. If you had come up those stairs fifteen minutes earlier you would have gotten to see me drop the prisoner in front of Commandant Ford's door. The reason that I have on only this rag" he said gesturing to the shorts he was wearing "Is because I flew all the way home so that I could see you all the sooner. The reason I smell like this is because I haven't had a bath in a long while."

"But…" Amber was about to protest but Jade did not give her the chance.

"I'm going to take a bath. Can I see you later?" Jade said putting his finger to Amber's lips shaking his head

"No" Amber smiled and kissed his finger. "You can see me now. You have been gone for twenty-nine days now Jade you can see me now. Since you have to take a bath I'll cook your dinner while you get cleaned up. I have every intention of coming with you. Do you have a problem with that?"

Amber had hands on hips and a stern look in her eyes with the sexiest pout on her lips Jade had seen in his life.

"I have no problem Amber." Jade said as he rubbed his thumb along her bottom lip remembering what those lips felt like against his own. "As a matter of fact, I don't think I could survive if it were any other way." Jade pulled Amber to him for the long awaited reunion kiss the kiss he had been fantasizing about the whole mission.

Amber turned her head just as his lips touched hers. "Jade you smell take a bath then make up to me that you were gone so long then get some rest and when I think you have the energy I'll kiss you like I've never kissed you before."

"You little tease" Jade said as he picked Amber up into his arms and carried her down the stairs. Amber laughed and the sound warmed Jade's heart. It was so good to be home or was that with Amber? It seemed to Jade at that moment that wherever Amber was, was home.

Commandant Ford laughed as he watched the exchange between the youngsters in the hall on the monitors in the wall behind his desk. Turning from the wall monitors Ford saw the solemn faced man enter his office, Ford stood and offered his hand.

Hell Found Me

"Administrator Gabriel" Ford acknowledged Nicholas Gabriel the Specialist Administrator and one of his best friends.

Nicholas Gabriel was the second most powerful man on the compound which could easily mean Nicholas was the second most powerful man in the world. The young man they were about to discuss could someday be more powerful than the two of them, that thought amused Ford to think that he was a guiding influence in the life someone so powerful.

"Commandant Ford" Gabriel said pulling Ford from his thoughts Ford began to shuffle through the papers on his desk. "I've reviewed the tapes from the satellite observation of the mission. Have you?"

"Yes" Ford nodded pulling the pictures from the satellite. "I've watched the tapes, read the reports, all but his, and looked at the pictures."

Gabriel looked at Ford gray eyes almost hungry. "He killed seventy-four lycanthropes sixty-four of those were military trained in under a week." Gabriel sighed sitting back in his chair. "Unfortunate the satellite could not show what happened in the tent, infrared screens in the canvas. All we know is that he emerged covered in blood. We have discovered the ultimate weapon our control of him will be a strangle hold on our enemies."

"Nicholas" Ford laughed to himself at Gabriel's arrogance. "Jade Hawk is too powerful to force into anything and too smart to trick into anything, unfortunate for his enemies but a good thing for us. His intelligence is one of his greatest strengths."

"He is young impressionable" Nicholas said deliberately missing the point.

"Don't underestimate Jade, Nicholas we do not now nor will we ever control Jade Hawk." Ford

Hell Found Me

remembered the scene in the hall from moments before with a smile. "That job is already taken, by one Ms Amber Knazze. Jade is most likely as we speak asking her to marry him."

Gabriel was in Ford's estimation overly surprised by the announcement.

"What? He's asking her to marry him?" Gabriel asked stunned

Ford just nodded as he absorbed Gabriel's reaction to the news. The emotions that played across Gabriel's face went from surprise to uncertainty concentration to calculation and settled on satisfaction.

"The Enforcers to be married I couldn't have made a better arrangement of power myself." Then as if a thought had strayed into his mind Gabriel muttered "Such an innocent looking girl. Well I have to go Commandant Ford." Gabriel said standing, as he shook Fords hand he added, "This union gives the compound more power than it was slated to achieve in the next twenty-five years. When they come into their own they will be unstoppable, the only way to contain them will be the twins."

When Gabriel left Ford's office the commandant let his mind stray imagining what it would be to control Jade Hawk, the most powerful person they had ever seen. After a short time Ford brought himself back to reality if the scene he'd witnessed earlier as many exchanges between Amber and Jade in the past were any indication, Amber had that job, for life. Powerful woman Ford thought having long since discovered what Gabriel insisted on ignoring, Amber Knazze, soon to be Amber Hawk was the key to controlling Jade, to control Amber was to control Jade. If the stern hand Amber used on

Hell Found Me

Jade was any indication she would be harder to control than Jade.

For their sakes Ford thought, I surely hope so.

When Jade opened the door to his dorm room he instantly wished that he hadn't. The twins apparently had not been back to the room since the last time he'd seen them a week before he left the compound. They must be living in the lab again Jade thought turning up his nose at the tangy smell that made his eyes water. Something he'd left behind twenty-nine days ago had gone terribly wrong. The smell of month old take out, garbage, and dirty laundry made his eyes water and his nose run.

"Jade!" Amber said as she rushed in to throw open the window holding her nose. "You should be ashamed." Amber ran to the garbage that was overflowing scooping up the nasty tidbits that had fallen off the top of the pile and handed it to Jade. "Take it away now. You are three doors from the incinerator why do you always have so much garbage? And don't you dare try to blame it on the twins" Amber said when Jade opened his mouth to speak. "They are never here so I know it's yours!"

Jade took the garbage embarrassed as Amber fussed under her breath and began to clean his room. Normally they spent their time in her room but when Amber did visit Jade's room she cleaned… and complained. By the time Jade got back from taking the garbage the smell, tangy as it had been, was almost gone. There was a strong wind blowing it out the window. The laundry was in a pile at the end of the couch and Amber was at the sink with suds up to her elbows as she scraped mold out of a pot.

"How do you work so fast?" Jade asked as he took in the scene knowing the answer to his question.

Amber controlled three things, fire ice and air. With almost as much authority as she controls me Jade thought Amber had conjured the wind that was now fumigating the room, used it to pile up the dirty clothes and had then gone on to wash the dishes.

Ignoring the question Amber only said "Put those shorts in the pile at the end of the couch, and by the way, this place smells and looks so bad I ordered in."

Looking at her with suds up to her elbows Jade could do nothing but smile. "That's ok love"

The one size standard Amber was wearing was wet and from the look of it today must be Friday. Amber had all five of her physical classes on Fridays. How she had managed that scheduling coo no one knew, but instead of having one physical class a day like everyone else Amber had 5 on one day this term and that day was Friday. Amber hated physical classes so she did the bare minimum to progress.

Jade walked to stand behind Amber, leaning against her he pinned her to the sink enjoying the feel of her small soft body against him. Taking the sponge out of her hand Jade turned Amber to face him.

"Amber" Jade said kneeling "I can't stand it any more." Jade pulled the ring box out of his pocket. "I need you in my life always."

Jade opened the box and held it up looking down at the floor Jade said, "I'm a mess, but you, you make me more than any man could ever hope to be. Will you please, please marry me?" Jade waited looking at the floor Amber hadn't moved or said a word. "Amber, please be my wife" when there was still no response Jade looked up to see Amber with her hand to her mouth nodding tears flowing from her eyes.

"Yes?" Jade asked.

Amber looked him in the eyes and mouthed the word yes.

"YES" Jade shouted jumping up from his knees lifting Amber into his arms swinging her around.

Amber laid a tear filled face to his ear and whispered "Don't you ever leave me there is no one else there can never be anyone but you." Then she kissed his neck.

Jade put Amber down and slid the ring on her finger.

"Never, I'll be yours until the day I die and then forever more." Jade lifted Amber's chin and looking into those golden eyes could not see living without her. When he bent to kiss her there was nothing in his mind or heart but her lips.

6 MONTHS LATER

The sound of the phone ringing pierced the silence of night Doctor Carlos Reas reached over lifting the receiver from the cradle and glanced at the clock. It was 2:45 am.

"Hello" He said lacing his voice with the disgust he felt for being awakened at this time of the morning.

"Hello Doctor," The voice responded smoothly, either indifferent to his disgust or oblivious to it. "There is work."

"Understood" Doctor Reas responded.

Hell Found Me

The never before seen contact was a nagging enigma, though Doctor Reas one of the most powerful telepaths on the compound, had contact with this man on a regular basis his mind was a blank unreadable space it was almost as if the man did not exist. The fact that they only spoke over the phone had nothing to do with the fact that he could not be read this was something…different, even if he was a powerful enough telepath to keep Reas out of his mind Reas should still sense his presence.

"You will receive the details within forty-eight hours." The contact said, as Doctor Reas for the thousandth time tried to read him or at the very least sense him at the other end of the line.

"Understood" Reas answered.

Again the attempt was unsuccessful Carlos Reas hung up the phone and laid back looking into the darkness above him. Who was this man? Why couldn't he sense him? Well no matter, if ever any one of their deals were to fall through the world would not be big enough to hide. Reas may not be able to sense him over the phone but they had conducted enough business that if the need arose Reas was sure he could be found.

3 MONTHS LATER

Katherine looked nervous.

"Doctor Thompson" Reas said trying to shake her out of the daze she kept drifting into. "What do you think of the plan?"

Reas was also trying not to be angry. If he got angry she would know and that was a problem he did not need at this moment. He resented the fact that he had to hide his emotions around her, almost as much as he resented the Evans twins.

"I don't know." Doctor Thompson finally said removing her glasses to pinch the bridge of her nose. "You know that I have reservations about this. I don't think that we should even try this. If we don't pull it off the repercussions will be disastrous." She shook her head as she replaced her glasses. "There is no way he'll go for this. If he doesn't we'll have put ourselves out on an unnecessary limb. Even if he does say yes she is definitely going to say no".

Reas could tell that Katherine was wavering but he could not, would not give up now so close to the end. They were so close to the big pay off.

"This has got to work. It's not like he has any moral high ground to stand on. This client has film footage of him in action. Without him they may refuse to continue do business with us at best they will not be willing to make the same offer for anyone else that we currently have on staff. They want to put him on retainer for God's sake."

Katherine looked away.

"Do you know what they're offering for him?"

Doctor Thompson did not respond to him or even look his way.

"Katherine!" He grabbed her shoulder, forcing her to look at him. "The time has passed for any pretence of abhorrence of what we do, what we have become. You know as well as I do that it is too late for us to stop now."

"I know," she said forcefully. "And believe me Carlos, I sleep well at night. But this is a life that I chose the others in the group chose this. I have no problem with that. But I don't think... No let me change that... I know no good will come of forcing, or tricking someone into doing these things. This is a road one has to choose for themselves."

Doctor Carlos Reas looked at the tall skinny brunette sitting across from him and shook his head. For his plan to work she had to go along. He resented the fact that he needed her and he let the emotion seep through, not caring if she picked up on it. She was wavering in her commitment to the cause, the cause that the two of them had founded and pioneered together. So he did the only thing he could think to do to bring her back to him he referred to the reason she had come to him in the first place.

"They have offered 1 billion dollars to retain his services and triple the normal rate for any active assignments he must take on."

Greed

Dr Thompson who had been looking at a spot on the wall behind him was instantly focused, dull eyes had cleared.

"Tell me this plan of yours again. We want to be sure that it will work."

Reas smiled. Greedy, greedy woman he said to himself as he once again told her his plans.

Hell Found Me

3 MONTHS LATER

The bachelor party was nowhere near dying down. Jade glanced at the clock as he walked past the bedroom, 1:30 am. Robert saw him from downstairs.

"Jade" Robert called "Anything wrong?"

"No" Jade called down glancing at the clock once again.

"Come on down Mr. Amber Knazze" Someone called up Jade looked to see one of the Evans twins standing beside Robert at the foot of the stairs. "There is someone here to see you." the twin said with a grin.

Jade had to smile "If it is a stripper I'm not allowed." Their response to that made his smile transform into a large grin. "I promised Amber."

There was a crowd at the foot of the stairs by that time and Jade's last comment was received by a rousing chorus of boos. Four men came up the stairs and brought him down for the show, which he had to admit, was quite good aside from the fact that the dancer wore a mask he assumed so no one would recognize her the next day. Was she an outside stripper snuck in or was she someone from the compound? Jade wondered. If she was from the compound then that would explain the mask, and for that matter there was no way they could get a stripper past the entrance guards but they could have gotten a permit for the special occasion it wasn't like the twins couldn't wipe her mind of anything she saw.

By the time the show was over the woman wore nothing but baby oil and the mask. Jade's clothes had splatters of baby oil on them and he had to calm his nerves. By that time Jade couldn't care less about the fact that she wore a mask or where she came from. The woman left shortly after the show and the party began to die down.

"Robert" Jade called "Would you mind doing me a favor please?"

"Sure what's up?" Robert said as he brought his enormous body up the narrow stairway.

"I was wondering if you would help me put some of the furniture together… the bed at the very least. I just got the housing assignment yesterday and I at least want to have a bed to sleep in on my wedding night." Jade looked at the clock as they entered the bedroom the wedding was supposed to begin at 8 am.

Robert saw him looking at the clock and patted his shoulder. "Four hours twenty minutes and counting are you nervous?" he asked.

"Not really" Jade answered leaning against the wall. "To be honest I can't wait. It feels like my life is set to begin tomorrow. I love Amber so much I can't describe it. The thing that I'm worried about is that something will happen to make her mad and she'll decide not to marry me or even worse after the wedding something will happen and she will leave me and never want to see me again." Jade clutched his stomach bending forward at the thought of Amber leaving him, the raw emotion Jade felt for Amber was more than he could describe. "I don't want her to stop wanting me if I loose her, I'll just die."

Jade had never known that he could love like this that anyone could love like this it made him afraid it made him feel vulnerable. "I'm also afraid I'll be late in the morning and she'll kill me in this pretty little house that we haven't finished moving into."

Hell Found Me

Robert laughed and patted his shoulder once again "Well there is one thing that I can tell you that will hopefully make you feel better. Amber loves you more than you love her, I don't know how that's possible, but she does. Everyone knows that the two of you are meant to be together and will be together for all time. The idiots that don't understand that are just... To be honest," Robert said shaking his head. "I'm jealous. Come on let's get your bedroom room ready for the little woman."

The Evans twins came up and helped them put the bedroom set together. Soon after 5 am they said their goodbyes and were on their way home. Jade too excited to sleep went downstairs and tried to put the entertainment center together. It might be nice to have more than one room in the house that was almost livable.

At 7:10 am the entertainment center was still giving Jade the flux but it was time to go get married. The knock at the door let him know the groomsmen had come to help him get ready and to the banquet center on time.

Amber had put the word out to Jade and all of his friends that if he was late or if there were any problems with her wedding getting started on time or any problems in general she would kill them all slowly Jade and all his friends believed her.

Just before the wedding Doctor Reas came to Jade smiling.

"My favorite student" Reas said "I think it is the first time I've ever seen you nervous. Are you actually sweating? Don't tell me that you have cold feet."

"No cold feet" Jade said "Just a little nervous."

Jade then began to fidget with his ti. Doctor Reas went to the water cooler and came back, handing Jade a cup.

"Yuck" Jade said trying to give him the cup back. "The water is warm."

"I know" Doctor Reas said as he pushed the cup back to Jade's lips. "Drink it all its good for your nerves." Jade drank the water while Doctor Reas fixed his tie. The wedding began, only thirty-five minutes late.

Jade stood at the front of the banquet hall breathing slowly, deeply. The wedding march had begun shortly before. There were only three bridesmaids and three groomsmen. The small chamber group began to play Here Comes the Bride and the whole room turned to see her entrance.

What an entrance it was! There was a collective gasp when Amber stepped into view followed by murmurs of how beautiful she was. Robert and the Evans twins reached over to pat him on the back and even the Reverend performing the ceremony nodded his approval.

Jade turned back to watch Amber as she approached him.

Amber's dress was golden brown. The top looked like a golden satin corset with gold embroidery worked throughout. It laced up the front and tied at the top between the swell of her breasts. The skirts came flowing from the bottom of the corset long satin skirts hung to her ankles in the front but trailed behind her in the back. The veil was golden lace through which he could see hints of her full lips smiling nervously... she was biting her lip. The veil hung to her shoulders, apparently clipped to her hair or behind her ears because Jade could not see how it was attached. Her head showed only her long brown hair arranged in spiraling curls that flowed from the top of her head like a waterfall. She wore golden brown slippers on her feet.

By the time Amber reached Jade and Commandant Ford handed her over to him Jade had come to the conclusion that this miracle of a girl would own him for the rest of his life. Jade accepted the fact that he would be her willing slave with a smile on his face and her in his heart.

Jade stared at Amber as the Reverend spoke.

"Jade" The Reverend calling his name stirred Jade from his trance.

"Hum" Jade stammered "I can kiss the bride now?" Jade asked as he reached for the veil.

The Reverend laughed and Amber's eyes went wide.

"I'll take that as an I do." The Reverend said.

"Oh, oh," Jade stammered. "I do, I do."

Jade was embarrassed and decided not to look at Amber again until the ceremony was over. That way he could pay attention to what was going on and not make any more mistakes. Fortunate for him the wedding went quickly after that, or at the very least there were no more mistakes.

"Now Jade" The Reverend said with a smile "You may kiss your bride"

Jade turned to Amber hugging her tightly he whispered into her ear.

"I'm your slave for life. I would die for you. Please don't hurt me."

Removing the veil Jade kissed his wife, and that kiss, the first kiss of his marriage to his body his mind

63

and his soul felt like the first kiss of his life, like water to a man in the desert. Stepping back licking his lips as he did so Jade picked Amber up holding her in his arms like a child Jade turned to the crowd of their peers and yelled, not too calmly.

"MY WHIFE" The crowd began to cheer as Jade walked out carrying Amber in his arms.

"Jade Marcus Hawk" Amber said as they stepped out of the banquet hall into the corridor that led to the larger room where the reception would be held. "Put me down right now!"

As Jade eased Amber down to the floor something told him that she was angry and that he was, not for the last time in their marriage in trouble.

"I'm sorry Amber, it's just that I'm so…"

"Jade" Amber cut him off. "I'm not angry with you. I love you, and I would never ever mistreat you or hurt you. Now come on let's see what we got."

"Wait" Jade said grabbing her arm.

The wedding guests were passing them on their way to the reception area. Some wanted to stop and congratulate them but most had the decency to know that the couple wanted a little privacy. Jade was looking towards the future, more importantly that night.

"The reception is scheduled to last four hours and could go on for hours beyond that. So I have an idea. Let's say we give ourselves a cutoff time. It's…" Jade checked his watch "12:45 now. Let's say we stay no later than 5:30. We'll sneak out and meet at the house by 6:00."

"Agreed" Amber, said smiling.

"Good" Jade said smiling back "I have a surprise for you."

Hell Found Me

Pain

Kisten stood over the... he did not have the words for what it was. With his senses dulled as they were and his mind in a thick fog Kisten could only struggle with the effort to breathe to make his heart beat to live, if that's what it could be called.

Kisten's sight took in the multi layered grey of the pile at his feet, no not at his feet, he was on his knees. When had they become weak? Or had they as the rest of his body numbed themselves? He thought of trying to stand but what would have been the point the world held no color and the... whatever it was had no smell or feel.

You're lucky, the words came to him as on a breeze and because the world held no sound Kisten was sure he had not heard anything but that some small part of him was remembering words spoken before his senses shut themselves down to the bare minimum to keep his body far enough from death that one day he could live again... If he chose to.

If I choose to, Kisten thought. Right now at this moment I could stand, if I choose to. But why? What would be the point? Is there some place to go, some benefit of this action? Is there some benefit to this life? Looking at the pile of ... directly in front of his eyes Kisten let the earth on the side of this face become the pillow that would catch the thoughts of his dulled mind as his eyes drifted shut.

"You're lucky," Kisten had been told by his brother when they were boys on their first hunting trip with their uncle. "You're blind to color so you can't see the vividness of the death in front of you. To have duller senses like you," Kisten's brother Kristian had said wistfully as his face normally a pure pale grey became the same grey as the ashes in the hearth.

"You're lucky," he had told his brother in his usual detached voice. "To see all the vivid things life and death have to offer. You know the sun as more than a glaring circle in the sky on some days and a bright ball in the sky on others." Funny that as a child Kristin had envied Kisten not knowing the red of blood and as a man Kisten resented Kristin knowing the red of a woman's hair. How priorities change with the years.

Looking at the pile Kisten had somehow curled himself around he thought to his brother Kristin, you're the lucky one.

Kisten thought back to later hunting trips and wondered at the ease with which Kristin had killed and skinned animals cut the small bodies of rabbits into even smaller chunks for stew or skewers. Resisting the urge to bury his face in the mound inches from his eyes Kisten marveled at the memory of his brother's strength. Though as a boy the site of blood and flesh turning to meat had for a while pushed Kristin away from the family's favorite dishes Kristin had soon returned with a new respect for his mother and her cooking.

Never knew that something so chilling could be made to something so beautiful Kristian had told their mother on the 10th night after their return from the first of a lifetime of hunting trips. This 10th nigh the one that Kristin's stomach had betrayed his color blessed eyes and forced him to eat the rabbits his mother herself had caught skinned prepared and cooked for them. Kristin's favorite meat in his favorite way smothered in onions.

67

"Thank You mother," Kisten had whispered to her over his brothers bowed head as grace was spoken. 'He was broken inside somehow' Kisten had told her earlier that day. It is an easy thing to fix had been her smiling carefree response.

Kisten's mother and his brother had been the only reasons that he missed and in turned did not miss the sight of color. His mother had red hair he had been told, but she had eyes clear like glass in blue. That he had seen, as he had seen the color of his brother's eyes were golden. The color of the eyes of his most loved had been the only color his eyes could see. He knew the names of these colors because he had heard them spoken. Many had told his brother that his tawny golden eyes were like the miracle of a sunset. And that his mother's eyes were the blue of the sky, and that was why his eyes were the gray of clouds on a summer day.

You are the lucky one. Kisten told his brother as he with eyes closed hugged close the one thing that he had loved as much as his mother, and after her death had become the one thing he loved. You are the lucky one.

The pile of flesh that he hugged to him was nothing like the strong beautiful brother he had loved. It did not laugh deeply with robust voice that made him happy that he was colorblind and not deaf. The disjointed skinned pile in his arms did not sparkle with the brilliance that some used to describe the sun. The pile was just there. No life, no love, no voice, just meat, meat with no smell or warmth.

How could Kristin have become this? Kisten wondered as he held the memories of warmth and love close to him, building the ship that would peacefully take him to where his brother and his mother waited for him. He was sure that when the time came that he saw them

Hell Found Me

again he would know the red of his mother's hair that had not in life had time to change to the dull grey that he saw it as, or his brothers red gold hair that all said matched his, as his face did identically.

If not for the difference in the color of your eyes no one would be able to tell you apart their uncle had told him. But the two of them believed their mother when she spoke of the many differences in their faces. There are so many unique things in each of you your differences astound me. How is it possible to be so similar and yet so very, very different?

The day their mother had died had been one of the most painful in his life. Kisten could feel his inside being torn to pieces and instead of dieing his body continued to live and be torn. His brother had lay in bed and held him close. The two of them had laid in their mother's bed for three days holding each other basking in her scent. They were numb to the world, numb as he was now.

Why did she die? They had asked not each other but the world. There was no reason to it, no cause. They left the house that morning and when they came home she was sitting in her favorite chair lifeless. The two had not wanted to move her or to admit that she was gone, though they felt the lack of life as soon as they walked into the house. At the age of 13 they were left with nothing but each other, and that had from that moment forward been enough.

Now 10 years later Kisten was alone in a world that not only held no color but also no light no love no warmth and soon no life. The world was nothing but pain. Pain made the world go around. Pain made people do horrible things to themselves and each other, and pain would take him from this world and reunite him with his lost family.

Kisten closed his eyes and held his brother's torn remains close to him. Wrapping his mind around what had happened to his brother, the horror that the one he loved would be killed skinned and turned into so much meat. The thought that his brother was now nothing more than what would be left of a goat gone to slaughter aided him in letting himself slip away. Soon there was nothing in Kisten's mind heart or existence but grey pain and darkness.

Donna was sick and she was scared. The pitiful excuse for an escape plan had almost gotten her killed, if she hadn't fallen into the ice cold water off the cliffs by the grace of the gods missing all the jagged rocks on her way down she would be dead. Now in the cold of the night she traveled through unknown forests. Is this what I was destined for? Was I born to die cold and alone in a forest? I refuse to believe that. Hurrying in what she was sure were circles Donna came to a clearing that once she entered it held a stench that made her gag.

Something must have died here, she thought as she turned to leave but decided to stay instead, tearing a piece of cloth from her under dress she covered her nose and moved closer to the smell that was causing her eyes to sting. It will hide my sent. She told herself. The dogs would not dare come near here. What she saw in the center of the clearing would have ripped a terrible scream from her throat if not for the fact that she choked on the stench of it when she inhaled deeply to breathe.

Hell Found Me

Pain

Lying in the middle of the of the clearing was what looked like a several rabbits that had been torn to shreds and then thrown into a pile about 3 feet high and 2 feet wide. Disturbing as the sight of the decaying animals was the man cradling it with his body as if it were something more precious than the long dead remains of animals.

He died cradling animal remains, she thought in horror. Why would he wrap himself around that gore as if it were something precious and then let himself die. Though she was sure the smell had not lessened the sight drew her in closer. How long have they been here? She wondered and she looked at the bloodied side of the man's face and hair. In the darkness of the forest night she could not make out his features but she longed to see him clearly. What manner of man would morn an animal so?

Kneeling in the sea of decay and death Donna placed her hand on the man's neck. She was not sure why she would do such a thing or when she had walked so close but the faint flutter of his pulse beneath her fingers told her that it was the right thing to do.

"You were going to die here." She whispered. "With these dead animals" why she wondered as she pulled his stiff body up, why would you choose to die in this way in this place? Mind racing Donna wondered how she would warm him, and how she could bring him back from the pit of the abyss that he seemed to have the desire if not the strength to cast himself into.

Donna pulled the lean form close to her, trying to hold as much of his body close to hers as possible sharing her heat and her will to live with him. After what seemed like an eternity she decided it would be better for the both of them if she were to put his back to a tree and

Hell Found Me

sit on his lap. Her clothes were still moist and the tree would block the wind that was wiping through the clearing with cold vengeance.

Once she settled his lean frame against the tree and settled herself into his lap Donna closed her eyes and began to plan the next move. She had helped this man and though he had decided that he no longer cared for life maybe she could get him to help her as well.

The fact that you don't care if you die or not could be a big help to me, she thought as she finally began to warm coaxing the small flame of life within him to the surface to warm them both. I could use your disregard for your own life to protect mine. With that the first solid plan that she had come up with from the moment she decided to escape the convent, Donna fell into what seemed at the moment the safest sleep she'd had in her life.

Kisten traveled. The pile of so much flesh that he had wound himself around before making the decision to follow his brother to the other side traveled with him. No longer shades of grey meat but his brother His twin walking beside him as he had all of his life.

"You're lucky" Kristian told him as they walked side by side, his golden eyes sparkling as they always had, but dimmer in some way, now shadowed with sadness. "You will be whole."

"You're the lucky one." Kisten told him as they walked, wondering at the sadness he saw in the tawny eyes he had loved and envied all his life. "You get to see the color of the world in all its warmth and splendor."

"You're the lucky one." Kristian said. "You get to live."

In that one statement Kisten remembered the dull lifeless world that he had decided to leave so that he could come on this journey and be with his brother and of course his mother. He would rather walk with his brother in death and even in darkness than live a thousand glorious lives.

"I will go with you." Kristen said thinking his words would take the sadness from his brother's eyes as the sight of Kristian alive and well wiped the numb cold from his heart. "If you are to die then I will die, if I must live then so must you. By blood…"

"You don't want to do that, not really." Kristian told him cutting short the pledge that would bind them for eternity. "I could not ask this of you."

"But you would leave me alone?" Kisten sobbed, "You would forsake me to colorlessness? You would leave me alone in the dark and the cold."

"This is the dark and the cold." Kristian told him. "You don't…"

"I was there when mother died." Kisten's heartbroken voice was now laced with bitterness. "Remember that time brother and imagine going through it alone." The last came out a child's plea.

"Brother, if we do this thing it will halve your life." Kristian told him softly.

"I have no life if you are gone." was Kisten's factual simple answer.

"Then with you I will come and together we will stay." Kristian told him.

Together the twin brothers spoke the words that bound them in blood and in flesh in life and in death. They would be together until they were no more.

Kisten opened his eyes in the forest and looked across the clearing at his brother standing in the spot where he had left him. When he saw the question is his brother's eyes he looked down at the woman in his lap and wondered what new world this was that his vow had taken them to.

"You brought a woman with you?" His brother asked. He had come across the clearing and was kneeling in front of them. Kristin's bloody tattered clothes hanging loosely from his frame.

"I don't even know this one." Kisten said shifting so he could get a better look. "But she has attached herself to me so securely... maybe in my haze... who knows. Do you want it?" he asked his brother giving up on trying to see her features and deciding that offering her to Kristian would be the quickest and easiest way to get rid of her.

"No thank you." Kristian said shaking his head. "Just dump it here and let us be on our way."

Kisten stood and the woman fell to the ground. The sound of her moan was ignored as he looked his brother in the eye and tried to scrub the memory of the mound of grey meat that hours ago had been his brother's body from his mind. Not wanting to think of how or why his brother had been killed Kisten just basked in the fact that his brother was alive and that they were again together, two halves of the whole.

"Hey," The woman said groggily. "The two of you would leave me here, alone and unarmed, in the forest." Donna tried to tie vulnerability into her voice make the men that were about to leave her alone in the predawn light of the forest feel guilty about her situation. "I am alone. I am afraid."

"And to us that means what?" Asked the lighter of the two voices that she saw were as close in sound as their faces were in appearance.

"I helped you." She said frustrated, angry now that the plan that she sketched out in her mind for the

Hell Found Me

man she found was being torn so easily apart by the arrival of his brother. "Before your brother arrived I took you from the mound of dead animals there and warmed you."

"Dead animals" they said in voices so chillingly alike it was like one.

"I…" Donna felt herself slipping down the slope again falling again into the freezing waters that would this time take her life. "I helped you, I am alone." Looking to the center of the clearing she saw that the animal flesh was no longer there and breathing deeply she wondered at the fact that the smell was gone. "There was death here. I am sure of it."

"Yes there was death here." Kristian said to her. "But death as you will one day learn is just the doorway to other life." He said looking to his brother. "If there is one of same blood and same life with love in their heart for you. There is no dead animal to be saved from here."

"But we do know loneliness and we do know loss." Kisten said remembering the pile of flesh that his brother had become and remembering that to him his brothers broken body had looked like the carcasses of several slaughtered rabbits. "This one time we will show compassion for flesh other than our own."

Turning the brothers walked the path through the forest that would take them to the road that would lead to the village that was the stopping post on their road home. The woman they noted followed timidly behind them.

She plots Kisten whispered in Kristian's mind.

She is afraid Kristian answered in Kisten's mind.

They sighed as they walked and wondered if the price of this kindness would be too high. The twins knew that there were those that would use their kindness as weakness. Though they were not what people that knew them would nearly consider weak there had been a time a time not that long ago in their minds that they were vulnerable. The time after their mother had died and they were unversed in the ways of the world. How quickly those around them schooled the young brothers in the ways of cruelty. The uncle that had loved and taken care of them when their mother lived was the worst of the lot. Many of the women that called themselves friend to the boy's mother had sent food for a while after her death Melissa ironically, their mother's least favorite associate gave the shelter that boys need after the death of a loved one, and saved them from the uncle whose greed almost turned them into indentured servants or worse. Glancing across at each other the men remembered being heartsick boys.

We were less than flesh to him. Kristian thought as he walked beside his brother. *We were nothing but money to be made. Flesh to sell to the highest bidder.* The memory shuddered him. If not for the fact that they were together surely they would not have survived. If not for the fact that Melissa would not allow them to be whored out to wealthy men from other villages they would be dead he was sure in a filthy hole by now. *I understand why you would not let me die.*

The walk around the village that they were visiting to the small cabin that the brothers had bought 3 months before was a long one and the girl that followed them soon became tired. Kisten was sure that she would catch a cold and most likely die within a few weeks if she did not find shelter and get out of her wet clothes soon.

"What should we do with her?" Kristian said aloud, he knew she could hear him and wanted her to know that they were not just two fools that she could

Hell Found Me

take advantage of. "I think that if she were healthy she could be of use around the house for cooking and cleaning, if we keep her."

"I don't know that I want to keep her." Kisten said trying not to smile at his brother's callous tone. "Then we would have to feed and house her, though now that the last cow has died there is room in the barn."

Through the entire conversation between the two evil men Donna had not said a word. She was sure that they were speaking of her in such a way to offend her and maybe to make her leave in a huff but she would not, not any time soon at least. They would provide housing and some degree of protection.

"I think that there are other uses for women" Kristian told his brother as they neared the last patch of forest that began their land. "Women can warm in the night."

Kisten's look in his brother's direction was one of shock. The woman behind could not see him and if she could she would not have feared them for the first time since waking in the men's presence that they would do her physical harm.

"I know that there are those that would think the two of us lovers of men." Kristian whispered so the woman would not hear. "And even lovers of each other. I think that this woman could be of some use to us."

"Brother" Kisten said in a hiss. "We came so close…"

"And she is not us." Kristian answered calmly.

"And we are not uncle" Kisten said the ring of finality cooling the air around them.

"Is she yours then?" Kristian smiled sadly. "One that you would love?"

"You are the only one that I love, will ever love. You are all that I have. She is nothing."

"Then why?"

"I cannot forget being small and helpless and I cannot forget that but for the kindness of one that we in times of safety never cared for would have been flesh whores. If not for Melissa…"

"She too is now dead and we owe no one." Kristian told his brother tenderly. Stopping in front of their house he turned to touch his brother's cheek. "The one woman that helped us even when there was no gain to it died alone in a house when we were gone from it for but a few hours. You know that I would not sell this woman to others, but I will not let the situation that we were in as children cloud our minds to what she could be." Turning to face the woman Kristian began to speak and noticed that her lips were blue.

"I think that we should take our new pet into the house and attend to it before it dies." Kristian said nodding toward the woman. "We will show her the kindness that was shown us once when we were weak"

Kisten pressed his brother's hand to the side of his face cupping it in his own. Though he was born first he had often in life felt younger, smaller and in some ways weaker than his brother. The thought that he had almost lost his protector and only friend sent a shudder through him that brought him to his knees.

"Kisten!" Kristian looked at his brother on his knees in front of him in heartsick agony. "You have made yourself weak saving me." He sobbed.

"Nonsense" Kisten ticked. I spent the night in the forest with no wrap and covered by wet cloth." He said nodding at the woman that had turned blue and was shivering so hard that her whole body vibrated harshly.

78

"You're sure?"

"I could not lie to you at the best of times and this is close to worst." Kisten said standing. "Lets get into he house and see to our new pet."

"And ourselves" Kristian added looking at his brother.

The small cabin was, the brothers thought more than spacious for the two of them Divided into two rooms one large outer room that held the sink oven table and chairs as well as the large hearth and two oversized and overstuffed double chairs. This was the family area of the house, where the brothers could sit and talk to each other about the day and about their plans for life. Plans, Kisten thought that had almost been torn asunder before they could even begin. Building a fire quickly as much for himself as for the woman that his brother sat in his chair Kisten wondered what the addition of another to their small family would mean for them. Would she prove to be worthy of their compassion? And if she did would they grow to care for and trust her as they had Melissa? But most importantly he wondered, if they grew to love her would she die, alone in the house while they were gone, and leave them with their grief once again.

It's the sad thing about women. Kristian said softly in his brother's mind. *They always die.*

Looking over his shoulder at the sleeping form they wondered if it would be best to harden their hearts to her.

"I think that we will be better for this, even if she were to die." Kisten said, remembering the contentment of being held in a woman's arms.

Hell Found Me

Pain

"Yes" Kristian said following his brother's train of thought into their mother's and then Melissa's arms as well.

The brothers peeled the damp clothing from the woman and wrapped her in a blanket and after building the fire so that it warmed the house they put her into Kisten's bed and climbed into Kristian's bed together.

"I would have died without you." Kisten told his brother.

"You would have been strong and you would have survived." Kristian told him, but shuddered at the thought of leaving his brother alone in the world.

"Tomorrow when we are settled in more I will ask the question." Kisten told him as his brother held him close.

Neither of them wanted to speak of what had happened to Kristian in the forest but there was a need and they both knew it. They would speak of this terrible thing and then they would deal with it in the way that was taught them by life and by Melissa before she died.

Settling in for the night together in Kristian's bed Kisten thought back to when they were small children. This it seemed was a time for memory, and he supposed that he should relax and let himself travel the road once traveled in his mind. There may be some benefit to it, to remember, he thought to himself, knowing that his brother could feel and see some of the thoughts that floated through his mind.

We were saved by one that mother would have once spit upon' Kristian thought.

Yes Kisten thought, *we were.*

Three weeks after their mother died and the boys were running out of food. Their uncle that had once come to the house often now came on rare occasion and

80

Hell Found Me

each time he came to the house he took something from it. This night was no different in that he took some of their mother's possessions, but was different in that he had three men with him that gave the boys an uneasy feeling.

"We are here to take the oven and some of the paintings." Their uncle told them as he walked through the house with an air of ownership he'd never had in their mother's life. "There are debts that need to be paid as well as taxes." Going to their mother's room he turned to look at the shocked looks on the boys faces. "I think that the two of you will have to find another home. This land in of little value and you cannot hold it. There are taxes that have not been paid in some years and it will be taken soon."

The boys felt a sinking feeling in their guts when he spoke, but were to stunned and afraid to question him. The sound of him tearing through their mother's possessions scared Kisten and angered Kristian. How dare he go through her things the boys thought to each other.

'Why is he doing this?' Kisten thought in his brother's mind. 'What is going on here?'

'There is something foul' Kristian told his brother's mind angrily. 'But we will think it through when he leaves.'

'He is taking mothers clothes.' Kisten told Kristian's mind in horror when their uncle came from the room with their mother's special dresses and shoes. The ones that she rarely wore.

"What are you doing?" Kristian asked their uncle as he clutched his brother. "Why are you taking these things?"

"I am taking these things to sell so that you will be able to live here in peace for but a while longer." Their uncle said mock pity in his voice deceit in his eyes. "But know that your time here is not long." Looking to the men that had come with him to their home he asked, "Is it agreed then?"

There were three men with their uncle each of them chilling to the boys in their own way. The shortest of the three was round and had a malicious smile that made even Kristian shy away from him. The tallest of the three had blonde hair and eyes that followed every movement the two young boys made. But the most frightening of the three was the other.

Standing of equal height to their uncle with brown eyes and hair the third of the men spoke. During the time in the house he had paid little to no attention to what had been happening around him. The boys thought him uninterested and had noticed no more than his entrance into the house, made more wary of the others through their actions. But when their uncle turned to him and asked if it was agreed his seemingly uninterested eyes snapped into focus.

"I will take them both." He said calmly looking directly at the boys. "They will do well in my care, if they are quick to learn and don't break to easily."

"But I would have them" The shortest fattest of the group whined. "I have the money on me to buy them right now. There need be no more pretence, no more lonely fear." Turning to the boys he smiled. "You do want to come with me don't you? You will be the most prized, most beautiful prized boys I have." Reaching out he tried to stroke Kristen's face Kristian slapped his hand away.

Pain

"Don't you ever touch my brother." Kristian shouted pulling his brother behind him. "No we do not want to come with you and you are no longer welcome on this land or in this house. Leave now!"

"Double the price for the one with spirit." The fat one said laughing like a child that sees a new and special toy. "I would like to have them both but I will pay the asked price for the one with spirit." Turning to the other men he said. "You can have the other one, I don't care for frightened birds."

"Now the deal was for the both of them." The one with the watchful eyes said. "I will have them both."

Frightened the boys looked at each other in awe.

'What is going on here?' Kisten cried in his brother's mind. "Uncle," he said aloud turning to the man that now haggled with the two more boisterous of the men while the other looked around the house as if he had nothing to do with what went on around him.

'Help us!' their young minds cried out in terror.

"I will have them both." The quiet one said. He had made his way across the room to where the boys held each other in fear and confusion. "They are now my property." Reaching down he grabbed both boys by the neck and lifted them from the floor cutting off their air supply. The fear and sudden loss of air sent the two children into a panic that quickly ended in darkness.

When the boys woke later they were in a room that they had never seen before laying side by side on a plush bed that smelled freshly washed, much like their mother's bed had when she lived.

'Where are we?' Kristian asked Kisten with his mind afraid to speak aloud.

'I don't know.' Kisten answered looking around with as little movement as possible. 'Where are our

Hell Found Me

clothes?' he asked his brother shuddering at the realization that though they were in the bed and warm the clothes they'd been wearing were gone.

Movement in the darkness called their attention to the corner of the room.

'Your uncle does not know how much value the two of you hold.' The quiet man's voice slithered inside their heads. 'How special the two of you really are, he doesn't even know that you were talking to each other right in front of us, or that you were going to run.'

Smiling down at them he pulled the cover back, aloud he spoke to them. "True that your young slender bodies hold much…" thought the room was dark they could feel his eyes on their bare skin like hands, "Much value, but there is more to be had here than physical pleasure." Letting the cover slip from his fingers to pool at the foot of the bed he watched as the boys clutched each other huddling in the corner. "If you can be taught then you may be spared, some things."

"Stay away from my brother." Kristian said. "You just stay away from him."

"You would offer yourself in his place?" He asked smiling. "You would give what I ask, so your brother would not have to endure it?"

"No!" Kisten yelled. "You will not have him." Though his insides clenched with fear and loathing he released his brother. "You will not have my brother."

"Such love between the two of you, such devotion." The darkness could not hide the evil light in his eyes as he watched the boys. "How deeply then does your love flow? What would you do to your brother, for your brother?"

The boys were again holding each other, holding on for life as they wondered at what would happen to

84

Hell Found Me

them at the hands of this man they had never seen before. How had they ended up here? What had their uncle done?

'Where is uncle?' Kisten asked. 'He will come…"

'Your faith is misplaced boy.' The dark voice slithered in their heads. "And don't forget that I can hear you." He said aloud. "Your uncle is the one that sold you. Sold you into a life of prostitution and slavery so that he could have the land and home that his brother's wife left to you and to him in the event of your deaths. Your uncle was always an untrustworthy bastard and was the one that killed your father."

'Father' the word whispered in the boys' minds as they listened. They had never known him. He died before their birth.

"I will tell you a short story before I take you." He said running his hand slowly down Kisten's bare hip reveling in the boy's whimper. "Your father was much like your mother, a trusting person. He worked hard and loved his wife and his stepbrother… oh you didn't know?" He smiled wickedly at the boys' gasp. "No Uncle was not your father's brother but his second wife's son.

"Your grandfather died a few short months after his wife leaving his son, your father to take care of the younger man, and leaving his fortune and his land to his only son, mostly. The house that your uncle lives in right now is actually your house his home on your land, and by saying yours your father's. When your uncle reached the age of manhood because your father felt responsible for him, and knew that he would marry your mother and leave the younger man to his own devices he let your uncle stay on the land that his father had left to him. He felt that it was unfair of his father to leave the boy with nothing.

85

Hell Found Me

Pain

"Your mother being the woman that she was
agreed that your 'uncle' should have something as well so
had no problem starting over with her husband. Their
thinking was that they two of them would have a much
easier time than the one young man alone. So they left
your uncle with a home and a piece of land and went to
build a life together. But your father's stepbrother was
not happy with the house and the land because your
father had the money. There was an account that was set
up by your father that he deposited funds into on a
regular basis but soon it was not enough. Your uncle did
not want to work and he was jealous that your father was
prospering so. When your mother became pregnant with
the two of you it was more than he could take. He knew
that if there was time your father would leave all the
money to his children as his father had and he would
again be left out in the cold so he invited your father out
on a hunting trip and arranged for a stray arrow of one
of their fellows to take your father in the heart, thinking
that the money would come to him as his brother's
closest relative. He did not know that on the day of the
marriage your father had turned all of his property to his
wife and was no longer the owner of the land either of
them lived on or even the account holder of his father's
funds."

The boys' shuddered. Uncle had killed their
father. It could not be true. Why would he do such a
thing? He had loved them so as children, this man was a
liar, he had to be.

"And why children would I lie to you." The man
asked standing over them. "You have no power here. I
can take from you whatever I want whenever I want. I
have bought you. And in my doing so have gifted your
uncle with all that you and your father had ever owned."

Hell Found Me

Pain

Reaching down the man grabbed Kisten's ankle and pulled him toward him.

"I will take you, first I think."

"Please no!" Kristian cried holding to his brother. "Take me please don't hurt my brother."

'Oh little one,' He said in their minds stopping their struggles. 'I will not take him. I abhor doing such things.' Aloud he continued, "But I must admit to sick fantasies. Watching beautiful twins together being one of them."

For the first time in their lives they were shown the thoughts of others. In graphic detail this nameless stranger showed them how powerless they were and what would happen to them if they fought him. He also showed them the sick things he wanted them to do to each other. As pictures of them touching each other filtered through their protesting minds they watched with horror, as their cries of protest became sobs of pleasure.

Lying side-by-side trembling in tears they cried afraid to hold each other, having seen their love perverted. Could he possibly make them… do such things, and enjoy it?

The sound of something cutting through the air punctuated by a dull thud and a heavy weight on their legs sent the boys into a panicked fit. They screamed and kicked trying to get the dead weight off of their legs. After a moment they were pulled up by the arms and slapped soundly.

The pain forced them to open their eyes and look up to the face of Melissa her features looked like those of an avenging angel with the light from the hall shining in from behind her.

Hell Found Me

Pain

'Come now quickly." She said in their minds calmly, but they could see tears and fury in her eyes. 'I won't hurt you.'

When she reached out to pull the boys from the bed they cringed and they could see the pain in her eyes and the fury of it warmed the room. The man that lay bleeding at their feet began to stir and they clung to her in fear. She would protect them, wouldn't she?

'Yes, I will.' Melissa said crooning in their minds and led the two frightened children to the carriage that she had waiting in the front of the large house.

That was the beginning of their new life. Melissa they learned was like them and the silent man that their uncle had tried to sell them to. Though they did not know if the cry for help that they had screamed in their minds before they passed out was heard by someone and that someone was Melissa.

She had come to their house and found their uncle there drunk and passed out in the middle of their family room. She pulled all the information he had on the person that had bought the boys from his mind and then killed him .forcing his mind to shut down in her anger. After learning where the boys were she went to the man's house and waited outside focusing her strength she put all of the residents of the house to sleep, making sure that it was as close to a natural sleep as possible so that she would not alert the man and have to face him directly. She knew that he had some gift from the part of the conversation he was having with the boys that she had overheard.

Kisten and Kristian had not know that she killed their uncle until they were much older and had learned how to glean thoughts. They also did not know until much later in life that the reason she and their mother had not been closer was because she knew of their gift and had informed their mother, and had given an offer to teach the boys to use their gifts that she often told them were not as uncommon as they would think. Their mother did not want to accept the fact that her children were different from most and had not wanted anything to do with anyone that she considered abnormal. She thought that if the 'oddity' was ignored it would go away. In Melissa's opinion she had left the poor boys defenseless and was to blame in large part for their sale and near rape.

Now they stood two of the most powerful men in the realm. Melissa had taught them all that their mother forbade and their life experiences gifted them with an emotionless streak that was in the eyes of many demon-like. Kisten and Kristian Land, together and bound by blood and oath no one could stand before their power and no one would get away with trying to kill or harm either of them. As memory faded to dreams they thought on how the mistake of not killing them both at the same time would be punished. Sighing the brothers let their minds wander to the faint sound of breathing coming from the bed beside them to the woman that slept in the bed and as their past circled them like sharks the brothers wondered if the kindness that they bestowed on her would become another source of pain for it seemed that all women associated with them died.

Pain

Hell Found Me

Twins

Thump, thump. Thump, thump.

Think, think! What am I going to do…What was that?

The amplified sound of TJ's heart was the only thing he could force his ears to hear over the roar of his blood flowing at a frenzied rate through his veins, as if it could escape, as if he could escape.

They're coming… What am I going to do?

TJ's existence had become terror and regret. Why had he not listened to the nagging in the back of his mind that warned him of the danger in that place? How could he mistake the malignant glitter in their eyes for anything but the evil that would eventually consume his mind his body and finally his life?

Got to calm down, got to think, TJ told himself constantly breathing as deeply but more importantly as silently as his panicking body would allow. As his heart slowed its attempt to force its way from his chest his blood slowly stopped roaring in his ears, allowing his hearing to ever so slowly return.

Thank God, he thought when he could finally hear something other than his internal organs trying to escape the mess he found himself in. The ringing in his ears that listening to his blood race had caused died slowly as he began to calm himself. Daring to look around TJ realized with dismay where he was.

He was hiding behind the same dumpster he'd been hiding behind when he met them.

"Thomas!" A shrill voice called.

TJ could not believe his ears... was his mother here?

"Ma'am you're wasting your time." One of them said smoothly

Oh no they are here too.

"You've been coming here for the past five years now." Another spoke kindly to TJ's mother.

"If your son is alive he's as good as dead." The sound of their false consolation burned TJ's ears.

"Who are you people?" TJ heard his mother ask.

"Everyone and no one" Was their truthful yet evasive answer.

"My son is not dead." TJ heard her say forcefully but years with them had taught TJ to hear the true emotion beneath the façade. TJ heard defeat in what others thought were the strongest of voices. TJ could hear his mother's fear just beneath the iron in her voice.

"Sure he is" another said, "He just doesn't know it yet."

"What are you talking about?" TJ could hear hope returning to his mother's voice, she had picked up on the implied threat and figured he was alive.

"Drugs" was their simple explanation.

"Yes drugs, they kill" they spoke to TJ's mother as if explaining to a child.

"But most of those fools don't even know they're dead. Their minds play tricks on them." TJ heard them mocking him but didn't have the courage to leave his hiding place to run to the safety of his mother's arms. TJ was frozen in terror he knew the threat they were making.

"Maybe you should leave." Again they spoke to his mother consoling understanding.

Hell Found Me

"We have things to do" explaining their presence in the alley.

Oh God!

"There are rats in the alley, they hide behind dumpsters." They told his mother letting TJ know that they knew exactly where he was hidden.

Oh God No

"We kill them" TJ felt his body go cold.

"Mom!" TJ screamed.

"Thomas" his mother called softly.

"Help me please." TJ cried.

TJ's mother walked toward him he couldn't see her but he could hear her footsteps. Crawling from the dumpster TJ looked toward the entrance of the alley and saw two of them smiling.

"You didn't really think she was still alive did you?" A leering voice said from beside him.

Defeat swallowed TJ before the others could reach him still kneeling beside the dumpster. Somewhere deep inside he'd known she was dead, years ago.

"She's just as dead as you. The only difference is she knows it."

"Funny how she died" A voice on his right said softly.

"Funny how we found her" another voice said from directly in front of him.

"But the best part was how we got the keys" came from behind him.

Looking up into their eyes TJ finally knew what had fascinated him about their eyes and terrified him. TJ had never looked directly into their eyes long enough to realize it in the past. TJ had always had hope for life.

They're dead

"To bad you're only just realizing that." A voice in front of him said as cold fingertips rested lightly on his pulse.

Thomas Jonathan Sanderson closed his eyes as numbing cold crawled up his arm and slowly seductively froze his heart.

"What about Timothy?" was the last thing he said. Opening his slowly dieing eyes TJ wondered...

The feel of TJ's warmth, his life slowly giving way to cold death thrilled and intrigued them. The four bodies that held two dead souls all trembled with glee as the life they were stealing but could not hold trickled warmth over their cold lifeless existence. As the last drop of his life force welled forth from his dieing body somewhere in their depths they mourned it's ending. Not the ending of his life but the passing of this thrill, the last of this treat. Waiting expectantly in the alley, they wondered why his death was taking so long. Hunger for the last of TJ's warmth ate at their cold existence.

"Where is it?" cold lips whispered in the night.

"Why does it not come?" another mouth of the same voice asked.

"This is not the place for this discussion." Another mouth said. "We will bring him with us and find his secret." A wicked smile curved two sets of lips, mirrors of emotionless evil "Stand."

Thomas' body stood following the command without thought. TJ was herded back to the small apartment that had been his home for the last seven years though deep inside the one bit of him that remained cried in terror and pain as his flesh betrayed him.

"What are you?" the question was asked as soon as the door to the apartment, and his fate closed.

"Dead" was TJ's simple honest answer.

"Not yet." Was the cool factual response, "But you should be."

"He does not know what it is we seek, so he cannot answer."

Had Thomas been more aware of the scene that played before his nearly lifeless eyes he still would not have understood that the four bodies that he had lived with for these past years were not only dead but there were only two people, the dead souls of a brother and sister souls that had somehow escaped their rightful place in hell by hiding in the womb of a whore.

In life they had been unearthly evil finding pleasure only in the pain or suffering of others. Their rebirth after death left them void of all emotion. Their cold souls only warmed by bathing in the life of others. They were drawn to Thomas like moths to flame something of him made them see reflections of the life that had eluded them for many years. TJ's selfish nature and lack of care for anything but himself reminded them of the life they had once lived. TJ's resemblance to them both physically and mentally was what kept him alive in their presence for so many years.

They had originally been born twins, one male one female. They often felt that they were only one soul, and each body carried one half of it. When they took residence in the womb of a whore they'd known and used in life they decided that they would be born again as quintuplets, that way each of them would be able to experience the opposite. Two female children two male separating their existence between each, brother and sister were now both. They played out their sick fantasies and lived lives no normal mind could comprehend. To be born with the knowledge of a lifetime, they thought, was a great gift they learned that to be born dead was a great curse. They could no longer feel anything, any pleasure or pain. Soon their malignancy grew to cold emotionless nothing. What a pity for the world, they could not be punished because they felt no pain. They could not be pleasured because they felt no joy.

"Something of him is missing"

"But what? What is missing? What part of him is not here?"

"Timothy," Thomas said the last of his humanity crying out in anguish as he betrayed himself for what he knew would be the last time. "Timothy is not here."

"Who is he?"

"My sister, my twin" TJ's body spoke.

"Our savior." four mouths said as one.

They now knew why they had been drawn to Thomas, why he had called to them like moths to flame. TJ was the key to life. They could use his body his life and his sister to regain their link with humanity, and in so doing their link to pleasure.

"Why have you never told us you had a sister? A twin?"

"It never seemed to be of a benefit to me to tell you" TJ said.

"Why are you telling us now?"

"Because I have no choice my body is doing your bidding of its own accord." Thomas cried inside because he knew that when they found and killed his sister that he would die as well. Right at that moment the only thing keeping him alive was Timothy's safety.

"Where was she when we went to the house to kill your mother?"

"I don't want to die" TJ keened.

"You're already dead you just don't know it yet."
They smiled. "Where is she now?"

"I haven't seen her in seven years."

"Where would she go if your mother died?"

"To live with our uncle Anthony in downstate Illinois."

"Does she care for you?"

"Yes she loved me more than she loved herself."

"Why?"

"Because our father died before we were born and I was all she had of him."

"Find your sister and call her to us."

"I cannot kill myself." Thomas had at the very least the strength to preserve his life.

"If you do this thing for us we will let you live."

"How can I trust you? You're already dead." His sluggish thoughts could not understand what they were offering him, but something in the back of his mind told him that they were offering him nothing but false hope.

"We will show you how to do what we have done." They told him smiling. "To be born with the knowledge you now hold." The four bodies advanced on him need radiating in their cold eyes.

For the first time TJ thought he saw something that had never been there before, an emotion.

"You will be what we are now."

"And what is that?" TJ had never seen emotion in their eyes before.

"Powerful." They whispered.

Anticipation

"Powerful" TJ whispered.

They smiled to themselves at the sound of hunger in his voice. It matched their own. The hunger for power they had sensed in TJ all those years ago now reared its head and gave them once again the keys to his soul and their lives. They would live again. They would inflict pain again, but most importantly, they would feel again.

"I'll call her now." TJ said hungrily. "But first you have to show me how to do it." He said catching himself before he gave them the keys to his future and had nothing to show for it.

"You have to find a woman that you've slept with. A whore is what we used."

"I've slept with you." TJ said looking at them with the faint trace of a wicked grin.

"It would have to be someone that is alive"

"We know that you have done quite well and there is one girl in particular that would love to bear your child. Find her the night that you bring your sister here."

As they told TJ the long yet surprisingly simple process of how to implant his soul in the womb of a woman he smiled to himself. He would be able to begin again. He would not be the first son but second fiddle of a dead man. He would make his own way. Being born with his life's knowledge would make him a very wealthy and very powerful man.

"You have to give me back what you've taken from me." TJ said as he walked from the small apartment.

"We will give you everything you need to complete this process." They assured him.

"You'd better." For some reason TJ felt stronger than he had ever felt in his whole life. Maybe they had given him some of their power in advance as a fee for bring his sister to them.

Hell Found Me

Twins

As they watched him leave they felt the cold calculation with witch he plotted his sister's and their demise. For the first time in over fifty years they felt the twinge of pleasure. It was like an eyelash on the back of your hand you could just barely feel it but you knew it was there.

"We will live again my sister."

"The key has been in our hands for seven years."

They would give TJ what they had promised they would let him have what they now had, become what they now were empty shells with the knowledge and memory of what they once were. They smiled with anticipation of the pleasure they would experience when they could enjoy the pain they were inflicting on him. They would live again.

"Tim are you ready?" Dylan called.

"I don't think I'm going" Timothy said.

"You don't have a choice cuz'. My dad will kill me if I show up without you."

"Tell Aunt Betty to call me and I'll explain. Besides we already missed the plane." Timothy said in a calm voice.

"What are you up to?" Dylan asked.

Dylan had felt responsible for his cousin from the day she had come to live with his family. Over the next seven years they had become inseparable.

Timothy had a fraternal twin brother Thomas who disappeared just over seven years ago the day before his thirteenth birthday. The disappearance came less than an hour after a heated argument between the twins. Timothy the female twin was born first and named after their father who died two months before the birth. The young couple had not inquired as to the gender of the child preferring to go into the delivery room 'blind' as they had called it. Timothy's father died not knowing his pregnant wife carried twins. The young couple decided that the first child would be named after its father even if it is a girl they joked.

Timothy was born at 11:56pm Thomas her younger brother was born at 12:07am the next day. So Timothy the oldest, and firstborn child was named after her father, even though she was a girl, and her younger brother was named Thomas. Thomas from what Dylan could remember was a spoiled pampered brat, and that was what had caused all the problems.

The life altering argument was over a gas powered go cart their father left to his namesake. Timothy who had given up everything her father left her which was everything he owned did not want to give up the go cart.

Anthony Sanderson, Dylan's father brought his small family to the twins' birthday celebration every year, so Dylan and his father had witnessed the blowup. The angry exit devastated Thomas' mother and sister, but it only angered Anthony and his son who saw it for what it was a selfish ploy to once again get what Thomas wanted from his sister and punish his mother for not forcing his sister to bend to his will.

The entire family fully expected Thomas to return in an hour to get his prize. Not his mother and sister, they instantly panicked and within 10 minutes had the entire family searching for him.

Anger turned to shock when hours of searching brought them back to the house with no sign of Thomas.

Timothy's mother sent her downstate to stay with Dylan and his father just under a week after Thomas' disappearance. She took an emergency leave of absence from her job so that she could devote more time to finding her son. The day Timothy left for her uncle's home was the last time she saw her mother, Timothy never saw her brother again either.

"Where are you planning on going Tim?" Dylan asked looking over her head at the packed bags on her bed.

"Home" She whispered looking at the floor.

Dylan was shocked "Where?"

"I'm going home." This time Timothy's voice held conviction. "I'm going home to get my brother, I'm going to make things right."

From the day Timothy came to live with him Dylan had been by her side. She was more like a little sister than a cousin. From the day she learned her mother had been killed Dylan hadn't heard her refer to the Chicago area house as home. His house was her home his father was her father he was her brother. Dylan was her family and her protector.

"I'll call Betty and let her know we can't make it." Dylan said. "She can explain to dad why we can't make it."

"I don't want them to know where I'm going." Tim said looking pointedly at her cousin.

"Like I'd tell them where we're going."

Looking down at Timothy Dylan could not imagine his life without her. It was selfish of him to feel this way but the tragedy had given him someone that he wouldn't have had in his life otherwise. She had been the breath of fresh air that brought Dylan and his father out of the cold lonely world they had built around themselves when Dylan's mother died. If not for Timothy Dylan's father would never have started dating again or married Betty. Seven years had brought them through many trying times together. Now they were in

Hell Found Me

college, and renting a small house together in the small college town.

Dylan was 15 months older than Timothy and over a foot and a half taller. He also outweighed her by well over a hundred pounds. Timothy was small her green eyes were pale, and sometimes looking into them Dylan thought that they were so pale a green that she looked blind. Jet black hair framing a heart shaped face made her pale skin and eyes all the more dramatic, and different from him.

Dylan Anthony Sanderson stood a staggering 6'7" tall and weighed 297 pounds. Years of outdoor sports had given him a tan that lasted through the winter, and bleached his hair. Timothy often told him his brown eyes were friendly and kept his size from being intimidating. The only physical feature they had in common were their dimples.

"We driving?" Dylan asked as he walked past her to get her bags off the bed and toss them over his shoulder.

"Yes," Timothy said following him from the room. "Your truck."

"No" Dylan said over his shoulder.

"Why not it's a long way and my car is old." Tim said.

"You have a reliable car." Dylan said sounding so much like his father it gave him pause. "Ok we'll take my truck."

"I'm driving." Tim said smiling.

"No" Dylan said as they walked out of the house. "And if you don't like your car why don't you trade it in and get another one. You can afford it."

"It was my dad's car." Tim said softly. "I just don't want to drive it this time."

Hell Found Me

Twins

To be honest Dylan loved Timothy's car and would be hurt if she were to get rid if it. The classic Porsche was kept in mint condition until she was old enough to drive and when that time came she barely touched it. Dylan drove it much more often that she did. Tim never complained because she loved his truck.

"One day you're gonna' let me have that car." Dylan said only half joking.

"I probably am" was her reply

The car ride was a long quiet one. Timothy was trying to bring herself to tell Dylan that this trip was not as much of a lost cause as she knew he thought it was. How could she bring herself to tell Dylan that Thomas had called her and he needed her help. How could she tell him that the brother that he had tried so hard to replace in her heart was back now and he would no longer have to play the role of big brother and protector?

Timothy loved Dylan but she knew that her real brother needed her and she would not turn her back on him and force him to leave again. She would not hurt him like she had all those years ago. She would do the right thing this time she would give him whatever he wanted just so long as it made him happy and kept him in her life.

Looking at Dylan in the passenger seat Timothy wished she could tell him the whole truth, but she knew Dylan would become angry as always when she tried to tell him about her feelings about her brother.

After what seemed like an endless silence Dylan looked over at Timothy.

"You know you could have rented out the house and made a little extra money." Dylan said as they pulled within the city limits. "A furnished four bedroom house would be a nice income property."

Hell Found Me

"Well I just didn't think it was right to rent out our family house. What if Thomas needed a place to stay? He should always be able to come home if he needs to."

Dylan took a deep breath he wanted to tell her that her brother was dead but he did not have the heart. Dylan had come with Timothy so that when her attempts to find her brother failed he would be there to wipe away her tears and shield her from the brunt of the pain.

"Look Timothy I just want you to know, whatever happens I'm here for you and I would do anything for you." Dylan said seriously feeling that was the safest honest thing he could say at the moment.

"I know" Timothy said as they pulled into the driveway of her old home. "I love you too." The sight of the house pulled at her stomach. Timothy hadn't been home in seven years.

"I think I should be honest with you." Dylan said as he shut off the engine. "I am not too sure that we'll find Thomas." He took a deep breath. "But I'll do anything I can to find him if he's alive."

Timothy looked at the window. "Thomas called me." She said softly not turning to face Dylan. "I never believed he was dead but I had given up on seeing him again. He called me last night and told me he needed me and that he wanted to come home."

The sound of the pain in Timothy's voice tore at Dylan's heart but he knew that he could not voice his anger.

"Where is he?" Dylan asked hoping his voice was neutral.

"I was thinking that maybe you should wait for me here. I don't want him to be uncomfortable."

Hell Found Me

Timothy said slowly still not wanting to look him in the eye.

Dylan took a deep breath they sat in the car in silence for a moment that seemed to last hours. How could Dylan tell Timothy that he did not trust her brother without alienating her? How could he voice the anger and frustration that had been building inside him for over seven years now without hurting her?

"I love you Timothy." Dylan said slowly. "I will do anything for you. The most important thing to me is that you are safe, and happy, more important that you are safe than happy."

"What does that mean?" Timothy asked. "You don't trust my twin?"

"I love and trust you and in the end that's all that matters."

"I don't want you there when we meet this is a time for family."

Timothy knew that her words had hurt Dylan and she regretted them as soon as they had left her lips but she would not take them back. She would be seeing her brother for the first time in over seven years and she needed to be alone with him. It was a private and painful meeting and she did not want TJ to feel as is he was being ganged up on.

"Well," Dylan said slowly. "I understand this is a time for family so I won't get in the way." The pain in his voice was like an open wound and he hated himself for being so hurt by her callous remark. "But I'm not going to let you go if you don't at least tell me where this meeting is going to be so I will know where you are and where to look if something goes wrong."

"What could possibly go wrong?" Timothy said finally looking at him. "He's my only brother."

"Who ran away seven years ago as a result of a spoiled fit and you haven't heard from him, now all of a sudden you get a call in the middle of the night. Funny how he knew just where to find you but you've never known where he was. Where was he when your mother was killed? For all you know he is on drugs now and planning on stealing from you."

"He can have anything I own." Timothy said softly and got out of the car. "And that includes my car if he wants it."

Dylan reached out and grabbed her arm.

"Where is the meeting?"

"Let me go."

"Tell me where you're going then you can leave and you can even take my car." Dylan said in a calm yet pleading voice.

"Fine," Timothy reached in her pocket and threw the small crumpled paper that held the precious address. "Now get out of the car I don't want to be late."

Dylan looked at the scrap of paper and then watched as his truck pulled out of the driveway and turned left at the corner. Timothy hadn't even thought to give him a key so he could get into the house.

When Timothy walked into the small filthy apartment her brother had been living in her heart broke. She could see that he had been living in squalor, and that there was drug use also.

"How nice to finally meet you." A soft voice said from a darkened corner.

"Yes we've been looking forward to meeting you every since we found out about you." The second voice sounded strangely similar to the first but came from a different corner of the room.

Hell Found Me

"TJ held out on us for a very long time." A different corner seemed to speak.

"But no one can hold out on us forever."

The strange emotionless voices frightened her but Timothy held strongly to her resolve. These must be the people that her brother had told her about. The ones that he owed money to and were threatening him. Why hadn't he come to this meeting? She now wished that Dylan was there his size was intimidating.

"I know my brother owes you money." Timothy said slowly, trying to hold on to her fear. "I have come to pay you what my brother owes."

"We know you are the payment." This came from all four corners of the room at once.

"What..." Timothy gasped.

Just as that strange statement was made Thomas walked into the room though it had been years and they were children the last time she saw him she knew it was her brother. Her heart ached at the sight of him. The girl TJ led into the room looked lovingly up at his pale features with a smile.

"I see that everything is in order." TJ said to the people hiding in the shadows of the room. "You have her. Give me what I need to have what I want."

"You already have it." They said as one. "And so do we."

"What the hell is going on here?" Timothy asked knowing the fear in her heart had leaked through to her voice. "What are you talking about? Thomas I came to take you home. I came to help you."

"And you are helping me." TJ said. "You're bringing me everything I always wanted."

The four forms converged on Timothy. She knew that she was in danger now and longed for Dylan.

Hell Found Me

Twins

As cold fingers closed over her wrists and neck she wished she could tell Dylan how much she loved him and hated that she had hurt him. Looking at the stranger in the corner defiling the unknown woman Timothy knew that she had left her true brother standing in the driveway of a house that hadn't been her home for over seven years.

"I didn't even give him the key so he could get in." Timothy whispered as ice seductively coursed through her veins freezing her throat. "I'm so sorry Dylan."

Timothy's life became a frozen emptiness Timothy knew that she had been given to these people by her brother. This was her punishment for driving him away as a child and turning Dylan away.

The two rituals began and ended at the same time. Thomas had implanted his seed and his soul in the womb of the young woman lying unconscious beneath him, and looking to his left he saw Timothy's body lying cold and lifeless on the floor. He'd had a will drawn up leaving everything to the child he'd just created. He had left everything to himself. TJ's joy could barely be contained.

They would be whole again. They would live again. In killing the girl and her brother they would have their bodies and their lives. Rising slowly from the floor they walked to where Thomas laid on the floor and touching his head lightly drained the last of his life from his body.

"It's done." They said looking across the room at each other.

They freed their souls from the dead husks they now used as bodies as if they were shrugging off jackets. The slender pale flesh at their fingertips served as new coats in winter. Slowly cold emotionless souls were wrapped in warm flesh, bringing life to a dead existence.

When Thomas' soul was released from his flesh it nestled in the womb of the woman he'd just impregnated. He felt confused for a long moment then he fell asleep waiting for his release into the world, and his chance to use his newfound power as well as access the money that he would get as Timothy's last living relative.

Dylan made his way by foot to the address written on the piece of paper Timothy had given him. He was worried about her and the fact that he'd left his wallet in his truck made waiting all the more nerve racking.

When Dylan turned the knob on the door and it opened easily his stomach sank to the floor. He was afraid to fully open the door but he knew that he had to. The scene before him confused and frightened him all the more.

Timothy and Thomas were sitting in the corner smiling and holding each other. They seemed to be happy to be together. That in itself would have been normal if it were not for the smell of rotting flesh that overpowered the small room, and the girl lying in the corner that appeared to be dead.

"Timothy are you ready to leave?" Dylan asked softly.

"Who are you and why are you here?" Thomas said standing.

"It's me Dylan." He said not wanting to breathe in the stench that seemed to be coming from four blackened lumps on the floor that appeared to be long dead dogs. "We came to get you and take you home."

Hell Found Me

Twins

"Yes," Timothy said smiling as she stood. "Let's go home. We have a long life ahead of us."

Something was wrong and Dylan knew it but he could not speak to Timothy about it. She had changed in the time that she'd been away from him. Who had she become in the space of one night? The drive back to the small college town they lived in was a quiet uncomfortable one, Dylan felt as if he didn't know Timothy any more.

TO KILL WHAT YOU LOVE

"Quickly, before they get away."

"But where, where should I aim? And how will the others know where to aim? There is too much unknown, too much could go wrong. I don't know…"

"Enough, there are always things left to chance. There will always be things that can and will go wrong. There is no need for self-doubt, proceed with confidence."

Anna took a deep breath and let all of her self-doubt flow from her with the exhalation of breath. She was sure that she would be able to perform this task, Hunter was beside her and his missions were always successful

"Now fire"

"Where," she asked trying to submerse herself in the calm water she imagined his smooth voice to be. "Where should I aim?"

"At them, aim at them."

"I don't understand" she said her doubt again trying to grab hold of her.

Hunter chuckled. "You do not aim in the direction of a place aim in the direction of the person or thing that you wish to hit. I chose you for this mission because you knew them all. You were their close friend. You know their voices, their smell, and their flesh. Take hold in your mind of the feel, or smell, or sound of them and fire at that."

"I don't understand."

"You were close to Connor, were you not?"

"Yes." I loved him from the time I was 5 Anna added to herself.

"Do you know the feel of him, the smell of him?"

"Yes," Anna hoped Hunter had not heard the pain in her voice. The feel of Connors arms around her had been what sheltered her from the fear many nights. If she closed her eyes she would be in his arms right now immersed in the smell of him.

"You're with him now aren't you?" Hunter asked smiling.

"Yes."

"Aim at him and fire."

"But…"

"You were with him just now, when you closed your eyes. Do it again aim and fire."

Anna closed her eyes and she was again in Connors arms, face pressed against his slender muscled chest. She could fell the vibration through his shirt when he laughed at something silly she said as he held her. Focusing she pulled fire from the air around her and lashed out, burning, destroying, killing her protector, her love.

"Anna Why?" She heard Connor's confused cry as he burned. Anna pulled away before she felt him die. She could not handle the feel of the death of her security.

She knew in that moment that she had done the worst thing she could have done in this life and that she would suffer for the rest of her life. No one could save her from this sin. As Connor died she knew that he had run away for her. As Connor died she saw his thoughts and his hopes. They poured over her like sand through open fingers. He ran away to try to find a safe place for

Hell Found Me

the two of them, mostly for her because he knew that she could not stand under the pressures of the way they lived with much longer.

"I see that your conviction is faltering." Hunter said calmly.

"No, I never had any conviction." Anna said. There was no emotion in her normally lively voice. She had clarity of thought and lack of doubt that she'd never had before. How could the murder of her protector make her stronger instead of weaker?

"You have forgiven him?"

"There was nothing to forgive." Anna stood. She could feel strength and calm flowing through her more potent than the blood in her veins.

Hunter smiled and turned to walk the three miles back to their settlement. There was no need to discuss what had happened. They both knew that something in Anna had changed and would never be the same again. Hunter had at the onset of this mission been her idol. She thought him the most powerful man in the compound, the reason that they were still alive. Now Anna knew how he made sure that all of his missions were successful

When they were in sight of their safe lands Hunter stopped and turned to Anna. His posture was easy and his face confident.

"You know I could use someone like you." He said in an offhand manner.

Anna smiled and to her it felt like no other smile she'd ever given. "Use me for what?" She asked.

"There are many that have gone out with us to find the deserters, and when the time came they could not kill their loved ones. Those who understood would not take aim, and those that did not understand choose

Hell Found Me

insanity and death when they realized what they had done. You are one of the few who could carry out the task and not let it destroy them."

"That is very kind of you, but I don't see where I would be of use to you. Connor was one of the few people that I knew personally. In killing Connor today all those that traveled with him have perished, and the few remaining friends I have would not run, they are weaker now than they were before and they will not risk leaving the safety of the homeland."

"It is true that most people become weak after the type of ordeal that you have just gone through but you for some reason have become strong. It is that strength that I would like to rely upon. I have ways in which one like yourself could become more of an asset than you would think."

"What is it that you want?"

"Your cooperation."

"In what?"

"You are an attractive woman. You would be able to endear yourself to many in the camp. I would not mind personally taking you under my wing."

"Are you saying that you would like for me to be a follower?" She was stunned, how he could ask her such a thing. She had just demonstrated her power and her ability to put personal feelings aside and take care of her duty and he had just offered her a position as little more than a whore. Who was this man that so many in her small settlement thought was a great hero?

"I would never ask anyone to be a follower. Though you should not look down on them, they are a vital part of the community. They are also very loyal and some would say that they have a power that most are not aware of."

Hell Found Me

Power, she laughed to herself. There is no power to be gained by lying on your back. Though the settlement was in view she was not quiet ready to rejoin her fellow loyalist. She would rather think for a moment outside of the walls of the town that she had always thought of as the safest place in the universe. This night had given to her a new train of though that she was sure would be best followed outside of the constricting walls of the town.

"I can see that you are deeply affected by what you have done though you try to keep a strong face. I will walk you back to safety then I will leave you alone. Think about the things that I have said to you this night and make a decision. There will be a time when I may call on you again and I would like to know that some thought has gone into the answer that you will give me."

Hunter turned and walked away expecting her to follow without question. He did not even look back at her when as she stood immobile and wondered at the arrogance of the man that had just turned his back on a woman that had just killed in cold blood on the words of a stranger the love of her life. Was he a fool, or was he that powerful? No one is that powerful she thought to herself as he disappeared from site in the security light of the settlement. He must be a fool.

That was a thought that made her wonder. How many years have I idolized a fool? One that would think himself so above all the others in the settlement that he could coerce me into killing the one person that she was sure loved me more even than himself and then turn his back on me without thought to what would happen. How ironic life was that she would learn so many of its lessons hours after she needed the knowledge the most.

Hell Found Me

If I not been a fool I would not have gone on this outing with Hunter but my lack of self and my weakness took me out in the darkness. I can thank my love for the lesson his death gifted me with, but at what cost. Though she had at the onset of the night been elated by the new feeling of power and security Connor's death had given her she was also sure that she would end in ruin. At the moment of his death Connor had grieved for her. Not for the fact that he thought that she did not love him, but because he hated the fact that he was leaving her alone. His sole mission had become her happiness and her safety.

"I killed him." She said aloud. The night as it always seemed to outside the compound swallowed up the ugly admission and it was gone. Alone outside the artificial walls that they normally huddled within she could admit what she had done without having to justify her actions with meaningless words. She did not have to worry what cruel intentions lurked behind the eyes of her friends.

"I killed the only person that loved and trusted me!" She shouted at the top of her lungs and she was sure that no one heard her, and if on the small chance there was another of the defectors still alive and they were outside the walls of the settlement and heard her words they would not care. Outside there was a feeling of freedom that the huddled masses could not understand. It was animalistic. It was primal and she would not let this new feeling leave her.

"Connor, if I had come with you then we would be able to share this thing in a truer sense than anything that we had between us in the past."

Turning away from the compound Anna began to walk. She was sure that this new planet that her people

Hell Found Me

had come to when the resources of their own overworked under cared for prostituted planet began to give up on its careless inhabitants would share many secretes with her that she could not learn huddled inside the walls of what was once their ship.

"How did we become so frightened and weak?" She wondered aloud as she walked in the night for the first time enjoying the feel of the night's air on her skin.

If we were a people so adventurous and careless that we killed our own planet and ran to take up residence on another what is it that we would fear? Why would we not set up house on this new planet and live to the fullest knowing when the time came when this as our home planet had died we could just move on to another world?

Her thoughts began to race as she looked up at the dim red moon with an appreciation for its beauty that she'd never had before. At one time not more than a few hours ago the sight of that moon would have foretold death. She would have been sure that there was a fountain of spilled blood behind its color. Now she was sure that the red was one of battle and strength.

The night was suddenly brisk.

"Connor," she spoke to the night. "If you and I had been as strong as our grandparents then we would have left the settlement together and made a happy adventurous life for ourselves outside the compound. We would have lived happily ever after."

Anna had walked so far into the night that when she realized that she was going farther and farther from the compound at a not so slow pace she was truly lost. She had come farther than the search teams that were sent to retrieve or destroy the defectors were allowed to go in what seemed like a short time.

117

Hell Found Me

Anna was lost and sure that there was no way that she would be able to find her way back to the compound in the bloody darkness of the moonlit night.

Sitting under a large stone Anna smiled. This would be her new life. She would make a way for herself in this new world without love and without company, but most importantly without fear.

Closing her eyes wrapped in her new security Anna began to drift off toward sleep, and Connor. In her dreams she would share this new power and security with him in a way that she had always denied him before he died.

"But why Anna?" Connor's voice asked her. "Why if the planet and the night were so danger free, why would they want to keep us in that prison? They don't even send the criminals out into the wild to fend for themselves, if one is beyond what they feel savable they are put to death. How can that be the way of those that have the best interest of the people in mind?"

Why indeed, Anna wondered. This must have been the beginning of the thoughts that drove Connor from the compound. The logic of the thoughts that floated through her head with the sound of Connor's voice could not be denied. Why would they want us to stay in that place? It was, she was sure, some form of prison. Though they were born in that place and had committed no crime they were kept in that abandoned ship like prisoners.

Well Anna thought to herself as she drifted off to sleep. I am now free.

The more the words swirled around in her mind the stronger she felt and the more she regretted that she had waited so long for her freedom knowing that it was

Hell Found Me

her weakness not that night's actions that had killer Connor.

The next morning a search crew was sent to retrieve Anna. Hunter had known that Anna would leave, like most of the others that had come before her. He hoped upon hope that the night's rouse would not take another of the gifted ones from them. He had even entered her mind and given her the illusion of killing her love and her friends when he allowed her to leave the compound as a part of the retrieval unit.

"How could you be so foolish Hunter?" The leader of the colony hissed. "She and her friends were very important to us. We will soon not have enough of the gifted ones in the campsite. The amount of power that you siphoned from her when she attempted to kill her love was enough to fill an energy storage tank. I will not loose my position because you have become ambivalent."

"Is there such a thing?" Hunter asked mildly. "I think that as long as I agree to stay here knowing what this place is and what we do to the people that live here I have shown that I actively support what you are as well as what you are doing."

"Wait, Hunter" The leader of the colony called to him. "Please don't be angry. I know what you are to this place, to me."

"I am not angry, and if I were it would not be with you I would be angry with myself." Or maybe I could be disappointed in myself, for being the fool for so long.

"Thank you, Connor"

You are to easily appeased the Hunter thought to himself. "I am no longer that person." Hunter said with soft reprimand.

Hell Found Me

"Not in a very long time, my love."

No not in a very long time. Hunter thought to himself. When he was sure that the leader of the settlement was not gleaning his surface thoughts he let down his guard and let his mind wander to the girl Anna. He waited until the guard was changing shifts and slipped out unnoticed from the campsite.

Hunter followed the path that he had ever so gently ingrained in her mind as he walked away from her the night before and found her where he had 'left' her, asleep on a large stone.

"I'm just glad that your love Connor and his friends did not take you with them last night. He is even more powerful than you are." Hunter told the sleeping girl as he lifted her from the stone to his shoulder.

Hunter carried the girl the three miles to the small hut that he kept outside the reach of the settlement and laid her on his bed.

"This is the beginning of the end for many. I am the reason that your Connor knows so much of the truth about settlement, as I am the reason that many were not killed in trying to capture one so powerful as he."

Anna opened her eyes to find that she had fallen asleep in Hunters rooms. This could not be, she was sure that she had walked far from the camp and had come to rest in the shade of a large stone, or maybe she had fallen asleep on a large stone she was not sure. What she was sure of was the fact that there was nothing of Hunter when she had gone to sleep.

"What are you talking about?" She asked aloud though most of the people of her colony did not need or use outward sound to communicate. "And why am I with you? You were gone and I walked away."

Hell Found Me

"And what little one would make you think that escape from me, if not the settlement was that easy?"

"Hope" She said evenly, but the look in his eyes made her turn away. "I didn't think I just acted. For the first time in my life I just did something that I wanted to do."

"That is a good thing. It shows that all is not lost in you." Hunter smiled.

"I heard your thoughts last night as I walked away from you. You thought me a fool for turning my back on you." Hunter said as he moved efficiently around the small room. "I am sure you know that if I focus there are few that can keep me from their minds, so what would make you think that I would not guard my back against someone that could kill their love in cold blood?"

Anna was embarrassed by the brazen thoughts that she'd had the night before and the fact that someone other than herself knew of them. She was not sure what the change in her had been but she was sure that some of it had come as a result of shock at killing Connor.

I am going to let you in on some things that may drive you mad if you are not strong. Hunter told her softly in her mind. For some reason the sound of his voice in her head was soothing and made her think of Connor. When her mind drifted to her love in the light of day she was sure that she would feel sadness and loss but there was none. It was as if the part of her that was carried around in Connor was still alive and well and she had only to find it.

What is it? She asked feeling a resurge of the strength of will she gained the night before. I don't know if it will drive me mad but I will not die the coward.

121

Hell Found Me

"First you must eat and bathe and then I will tell you all you need to know" Hunter spoke aloud breaking the contact between their minds.

"I would rather know now." She said settling herself to listen and read between the lines of what he said to her. She was sure that some of what he said to her would be false, and she was also sure that some of what he said to her would be true and would change her life in more ways than the event of the night before.

"Strong girl" Hunter said, "I wonder if Connor knows how strong you are. Or is it that he is the one that has made you this strong by sheltering you from so may of the storms that flow through the camp?"

"Connor called me his pillar of strength." She spoke quietly not trying to hide the tremor in her voice. She was sure that Hunter would know if she tried to hide from him so why waste the energy.

"He was more right than you know." Hunter said taking a seat in the only chair in the cabin. "This story that I am going to tell you will outrage you and it will most likely drive you mad. There have been those before you that were not strong as I thought they were and their minds broke with the truth. Others became the hunted of the camp because their rage at the injustice drove them to try and break the camp, and in doing so break what I at one time thought was the most important thing in the world to me." Hunter sighed deeply. "When I look at all the things that I have done over the years in the name of love it makes my body and mind heavy and my heart turns to lead."

"You are the savior of this camp." Anna said to him in awe. "Were it not for you and your power the camp would have fallen years ago."

Hell Found Me

The surety in her voice called to Hunter's anger like gas calls to fire.

'What makes you think that the fall of the camp is not a good thing?" He asked her. "Why in the world would you think it would be good for people to live in fear in the husk of a ship that died long ago, to make no advancements, to cower in the darkness afraid of the world and afraid of life? What is in your head that would make you think that was healthy, a way for humans to live? Why would you think it right for freedom to be a criminal action? Why would you think there should be none allowed to leave the camp? Where in your mind is this a good thing?"

Anna could see the fire in Hunter's eyes and could feel his anger as if it were a great fire that warmed the small cottage they sat in, what she could not understand was why. Hunter, the great one that protected the colony with the lives of so many others was now speaking words that were the highest of treason, punishable by death, by his own hand. Why would he say these things?

"I planted the seed of knowledge in your mind last night but it seems that you have slept it away. I thought so much more of you than this." His head lowered and a sound almost of defeat came in the form of his sigh.

"I remember my thoughts of last night. I remember wondering why we huddled in the compound, but I was not aware that those thoughts came from you. Please explain to me, I do not want to live in ignorance, no, in darkness any longer. Let the sleeper awake."

Hunter smiled at her words. He was sure that she would be the one that would free the colony as well as him. The sins of his past would no longer haunt him and

123

she and her love that happened to be his namesake would be the ones that would save their people.

"Think of this as a history lesson." Hunter said settling himself in front of her. "This is the untold history of the colony and those that govern it."

"Ok"

"As you knot the mother Earth was killed by humans. We in our arrogance and greed thought that the world was ours for the taking and because there was no species on the planet that could dominate us we eventually prostituted our home world to death. Pillaging anything we thought held value and killing or destroying anything that we felt did not including each other.

Eventually the knowledge holders, they were called scientists, saw that the earth would soon no longer be able to sustain life, ours or any of the other species that had survived us. They made this discovery and took years to build the ships that would take the inhabitants of the world off the planet. There were also expeditions to other planets that had some success but would not survive without the assistance that they were receiving from the home world. On mother earth there were large forms of solid water that they called glaciers."

"I know of the great water walls and how the scientists built large ships to carry them to the new planets so that the humans would have the precious water they needed to survive." She interjected caught up in the story of her history so that she was sure that she could almost feel the hard cold of the solid water stored in the sterile metal holders designed to keep the water solid on its long trip through space.

"Good" Good he smiled. "Then let me jump forward to the planets that had been colonized." He said leaning back in his chair. "The planets that had already

Hell Found Me

been colonized were dealt with in different ways. There were some that had more affluent people on them, and had been used as resorts for the wealthy, and then there were those planets that were little more than outposts. Planets were those people that were looking to make their fortune worked. Some of the colonial planets were little more than indentured servant camps, some no better than…." shaking his head Hunter continued.

"But the humans that had lived on the mother planet until the time that it could no longer sustain them took great care in deciding which of the colonial planets they would call the new earth and how those that were allowed to live on this new home world would be chosen. None were left on the home planet to die but not all had the same means to stake out their claim to a new life. Many of those that were what was called on the home world working class people went to the mining and agricultural planets. I could go on and on telling how the planets were colonized but I will put it simply. People formed groups and that is how the planets were colonized. All in this same solar system there are planets that hold our brothers. They have for the most part maintained the power of space travel."

"Are you saying that…?"

"Wait young one let me finish." Hunter said softly you will need to understand it completely. "After a while the earthlings, as they called themselves, that had kept residence on the home planet noticed that the people that had lived on the colonized planets for more than 10 or so years were different. Their children had abilities or features that humans did not have. It varied from planet to planet, but after two generations they noticed that the talents or features depended on the

Hell Found Me

planet on which the family called home. Mutation is the word that the educators called it."

"So we then are different from our…"

"Patience," Hunter chided softly. "On this planet, before the mutation was discovered there was a small mining facility. There were not many who colonized this planet, and those that were here though they weren't indentured servants were what the humans would call poor. In saying that you should now gather that the resources distributed to this planet were few if any. Those with what the humans called money could afford to buy what they needed and those with great minds would be taken care of so that they could make sure that the species survived and advanced. There are brother and sister planets out there that are utopias and great learning places. There are even some that they say are so like the mother planet that those who know the true history and have seen it with their own eyes can not tell the difference.

"There were those on this planet who learned of the pending disaster on the home world and tried to go back to salvage what they could. This planet could not survive without the resources that the home planet provided, so there was a small group of men chosen to go home and get whatever resources they could and come back. They did not have the means to move the whole colony though it was small, so they took the risk. When they got to the home planet all of the fresh water was gone and most of the trees dead. They gathered as many forms of plant life they could and seeds, but the main concern was water. They knew that one tree could become hundreds over time but without fresh water they would die.

126

"They decided that they would take as much of the salt water as they could and try to find a way to purify it when they got home. They also took as many forms of aquatic wild life as they could. But this trip due to the size of the condition of the ship and the size of the crew took many years. When they returned they noticed changes in the small children now teens that they had left behind."

"Changes? What kind of changes." She asked

"Well first of all, they as we do not need fresh water, but salt water to survive. So the ocean of water they brought home was perfect for their children even if it would kill them. But more importantly the children had abilities they did not."

"Please Hunter I don't understand."

"To be short with it. Our ancestors had no control over their environment. They had none with mastery of the elements." Hunter explained. "The power you used to kill Connor, is something that you gained as an adaptation to your home planet."

"I know that there are not many with the level of power that I have. It is something that Connor advised me to keep to myself. But all of us…"

"Now we do but the originals, from the home could not drink salt water just as they did not have any control over the elements, or the environment."

"But what does this have to do with the fact that we live like prisoners?"

"The control that you and your friends have, the control that is a natural to everyone that is descended from the line of original settlers of this planet is a very valuable thing. I am sure that you are not aware of this but the power that our people have over the elements is something that can be harnessed and used as an energy

Hell Found Me

source. There are containment generators that were developed by some of the originals children. These generators were created as a way to save their parents and family members that had not yet adapted to the environment.

"These containment units the originals then filled with their elemental energy. As they filled them they began to understand their power more and it began to grow. Each of the elemental powers were stored in a different type of generator and used for different purposes. The descendants of the original colonists used the power harnessed in the containment generators to terra-form, the planet and make it livable for their friends and family that could not live in the planets natural conditions. They made this planet a paradise. The ocean water that their fathers traveled so far in their ragged ship to glean, with its wildlife was placed and supplemented. The trees and seeds they nurtured to grow. All the wildlife that their fathers brought back they helped to adapt, survive and flourish. Soon this planet was as close to the original home planet as it could be, and humans from other planets learned of the adaptations and advancements made on this planet they began to come here to colonize here and to trade here.

"Due to the nature of the work that they were doing in an effort to save their loved ones the originals separated themselves from the others, the Normal humans that they loved so, and that loved them. The lifespan of our people is much different, longer than our human counterparts. Where you at 273 years old are still considered a youngling, you have lived twice the time of an original. There was limited contact with the outside, because the children of the colonists gained with their gifts a level of focus that the originals did not have.

Hell Found Me

"As time passed those with the gift, descendants of the original colony lost the memory of why we were doing what we did while those who were new to the planet. They did not remember the outside, the area we live in you see in the one part of this planet that is uninhabitable by humans."

"But, I still do not understand. I see the sadness of it, all the work of our fathers and grandfathers to make this place safe for the ones that they loved. But now that it is safe for them why then do we not go out into the paradise that we have created and reap the benefits of our work? We no longer fill the containers anyway."

"That is the issue." Hunter said. "And the great crime. We do still fill the power containment canisters. For the profit of the one that leads the camp and teaches the young ones like you that it is dangerous to leave the compound. The compound that is nothing more than a slave camp where natural abilities of the inhabitants are prostituted, much like the planet that gave birth to our fathers."

"But how we don't..." Anna protested.

"There was one who grew tired of the solitude and left this area, went to visit the family that he thought he was working so hard to preserve. When he reached the part of the continent inhabited by 'normal' humans he learned that his father and sister had died years ago, and that the new residents of the planet that had spawned him, were selling the canisters, for no small profit. When he found the truth behind their isolation, he was in some ways overjoyed that the work of he and his comrades was a success and that they would no longer be forced to live as outcasts, but saddened that his family was dead. All of them dead, nothing more than a distant memory."

The sadness in Hunters voice called to Anna. She looked at him eyes again regaining focus lost during the telling of his story. "What happened?" Anna asked. "From the weight of your words it must have been something terrible."

"He was seduced." Hunter said, and though his words were matter of fact Anna could hear beneath his tone to the bitterness beneath. "A woman with beauty the likes of which he had never seen approached him before he left. She convinced him that he should not stop the valuable work that they were doing, that even though their original family members had passed the children of their families were still there. She showed him several children that she convinced him were his descendants. She told him that..."

The sound of Hunter's sob pulled Anna from the vision she felt she was sharing with him. The feeling of sorrow that rose from him washed over her like she imagined waves from the ocean would.

"She told him that their efforts were keeping his descendants alive, and that they were the foundation of this planets economy. That if they stopped the children would starve and that in the end all the work they had done would be for nothing." Anna said pulling the words from his broken heart. "And he... You believed her." She said softly looking up into Hunters eyes. "He, you were hundreds of years old, but you were a child still in many ways. You had not developed, matured, none of you had, and your innocence damned you, all of you."

"I brought her back here with me." She was not born on this planet you see she is from one of the brother planets in the solar system. She can survive on

Hell Found Me

this continent, but it took lots of energy to maintain her until she could adapt." She then began to encourage us, them to mate, and have children of our own. Our children she knew would be the future. If we died without having children all the work she explained would be for nothing. Once the children reached a manageable age, the others began to die. I never understood why I lived while all my friends, my brother died. I loved and protected their children and their children's children, until I realized that she used my love for her as a tool to gain wealth and power."

"She killed them all, didn't she?" She killed them all and started the rumors that we could not survive outside the compound. That it was dangerous. She is gleaning power from us and selling it, and when we become inconvenient she has us killed, by you."

"Yes, I am the murderer of all my children and my friends. This thing that I worked so hard to make to save what I loved has become a testament to my failure."

"It is the leader of the camp isn't it?" Anna asked voice void of emotion. "She is the one that has turned us into slaves."

"Yes."

Why have you killed those that left the settlement?" Anna asked still numb, "Why would you make me kill Connor?"

"I have not killed anyone. Those that choose to leave I explain the truth to them so that they will be prepared for the outside world. Most break or try to destroy the camp, and in turn are killed by her. The others I have built a small settlement for them on the far edge of the continent that none but us can survive in."

"Where is Connor?"

"He is in the settlement," Hunter admitted. "I could not kill my only son"

"Your Son?" Anna was shocked.

"He is my son." Hunter told her. "He knows everything and has for about 150 years now. His mother was my best friend, the last to be killed by the monster that snared us. I kept him hidden and educated him well. He is at the settlement, waiting for you."

The joy she felt at learning Connor was still alive washed away the sadness and bitter despair she felt moments before. But, whose despair was it. She was sure that she did not feel the depths of sadness and guilt that washed over her a moment ago.

"Hunter, when you told me this story of your past, I could see it, as well as feel all your emotions. I know that you think it is your doing. That all the misuse and death in the camp is your doing, but it is not." She reached a hand out to him and for the first time she saw Connor her love in his eyes. Not that they had any more physical resemblance than any of the other colonists, but there was something of Connor in him, or was it that there was something of him in Connor?

"You are kind young one, but the truth of the matter is that I brought the serpent to the Garden of Eden. I am the one that killed the people that I had spent most of my life with and even if it was unknowingly they are no less dead. What made my crime all the worse is the fact that once I learned of what I had done instead of killing the monster that had in many ways imprisoned and enslaved my people I aided her. I am the one that siphons the energy from our people to keep the generators full. I am the one that allows our natural gifts to be used by outsiders. I am the one that is

Hell Found Me

killing us and this planet." The surety that Hunter spoke with made her only surer that he was wrong.

"And if when you learned of this treachery you had tried to stop her what do you think would have happened. Do you honestly think that the ones that she is working with outside the settlement would have been so easy to give up this profitable enterprise?" Anna asked him. "I have read all of the history books that are in the settlement. I know of how the planets were colonized and I am well aware of the history of the home planet and the Slavery that occurred soon after the flight from the home world. There are some that carried the misdeeds of the home planet to space with them and with none of the former law enforcement bodies on the planets and livable asteroids that they colonized the atrocities that were born on their home world grew to full malignant glory."

"No we could have…" Hunter protested.

"We could have what father?" Connors voice filled the small cabin.

"Connor this is not the…" Hunter protested

"This is the time." Connor's voice reprimanded. "You know full well that we could not survive a war with the outsiders. We know nothing of it, and have not the heart or mind for it. There are those that would not even want to leave the shelter of the settlement even if they did know the truth. I would rather my people live in the ignorance of their slavery and imprisonment that be mistreated and know that they are little more than lap dogs."

Anna sat stunned as she listened to the conversation between father and son. She was sure that Connor was alive now as she was also aware that he was more powerful than even, the Hunter.

Hell Found Me

"Connor can't you see that you are frightening her? It is why we hide our power. Most are not powerful enough to hear it when we speak like this but those who are…" Hunter said looking intently at Anna. "Come, my son"

"I cannot leave the village right now father. There is an issue with the irrigation tunnels and I would like to take care of it before Anna arrives." Connor said. "I don't want you to do anything to hurt yourself father. I still need you very much."

"I love you too my son." Hunter said in a stern voice. "But do not enter her mind and try to use her to voice your opinions, speak for yourself. You are not weak like me."

"Use my…"

Did you actually think that he had transmitted his physical voice here that it was an actual sound that others could hear? Hunter said in her mind, she felt his chuckle, no my dear his voice was in your head, I just pulled the layers of your thoughts from it like pulling blankets from a sleeping person." Smiling at her Hunter said aloud "I did not feel it was fair to you for you to voice his opinions and not know it."

"I see," Anna said. "There was a time when I was very angry with one of the girls at the camp. She is very pretty and I felt that she wanted Connor for her own. I wanted so badly for Connor to tell her that I was his love and that she had no chance with him."

Hunter's laugh surprised her.

"What is…?"

"I have always wondered where he learned that particular skill." Hunter said. "I never taught him how to do it, because it was something I only recently learned to do myself, about 75 years ago when he tried it on me." Hunter said looking intently at her.

Anna's face reddened because that was around the time that she had used that particular gift on Connor. He had apparently learned it from her. But how had he known that she had used his voice in that way?

"Though using others' voices to speak is a fairly new skill to us. I have always had the ability to detect others presence in my mind, as well as guide others into the actions that I want them to take. This was one of the first skills I taught my son. Had others known that he was my son he would have been a target and may not have lived past his second cycle."

Anna's face was on fire. She could feel it burning with the realization that Connor had known all along that she used his voice to speak. He had known all along and he had allowed her to do this. To tell another woman that she was sure was far more beautiful and more powerful than she would ever be that he loved her and always would.

"Because it was the truth." Hunter said softly. "He spoke nothing but the truth."

"He spoke the truth today as well." Anna said to the Hunter. "The best thing that you can do for our people is to let them continue as they are, and liberate them a few at a time. There may even be some that would stay knowing the position they are in. We have become very complacent. And these are my own words not Connor's it is better to live in ignorance than in Agony."

"If we learned to fight …"

"If we fought one of two things would happen. We would either become murders or we would be killed." Anna said seriously. "There are very few of us, and many of us are weak, not in our control of the elements but in our minds. If just learning the truth breaks the minds of most what would war do?"

Hunter sighed, knowing that she spoke fact. But somewhere in his heart he was sure that there was a way to escape this, a way for him to escape his guilt.

"Killing yourself in a last Valliant effort to redeem yourself will not fix this. It will make it worse. No one will leave the camp if you die, and it is a cowards escape of responsibility." Anna said quietly.

"Fire," Hunter hissed, "Earth and Air, you and Connor both."

"Yes," Anna said. "As well as all of our friends. You are the only one of us ever to control all 5 Connor and I control 4."

"Spirit, that is rare. You are dangerous young one." Hunter said sadly. "If you were not who you are I would kill you."

"I can read more of you than most. I know why those that had any control of spirit were killed, and why it drains your heart. Connor always shielded that ability sometimes even from me."

"All the power we put into those containers, it is the life energy of this planet. The elemental energy's can slowly if done carefully be replenished, but only if the spirit is strong. It is like the planet is a living thing, and the earth, fire, water and air energy that we contain are small parts of the body being removed. If the spirit is strong it can heal the body. You had no choice if they had the spirit of the planet we would all be dead right now, as would this world, and unlike our ancestors we are linked to this planet. I do not think we could live anywhere else." The look of shock on Anna's face when she spoke those words tore at his heart. She had just realized something he learned many years ago when he had forced the shutdown of the mind of a young man that held control of the spirit element.

"I will continue as I have. Taking the most powerful of us away from the camp." Hunter said resigned to his fate. "The village will grow and we will replenish the home planet in all ways that we can." Looking at Anna he made a crucial decision. "I have told Connor that if I die he is to destroy the compound. Nothing is to remain. With his power and control he could do it easily. Everyone in the village knows the truth and how vital it is that this is carried out."

"I understand and agree." Anna said.

"But now that you, a master of spirit will be living in the village, when a child is born with that gift I will take it to the village. The two of us can heal a lot of damage but I would like to …"

"Prevent murder" Anna smiled. "I agree with all that you have done to preserve us Hunter. Bring the children to me when they are born. As a matter of fact, all children born with gifts should be brought to the village."

"I have been doing that for years." Hunter said smiling. "Everyone in the village knows the truth, and there are almost as many people in the village as in the compound, the people in the village are more powerful, but they are mostly children, young ones who were taken from their parents as babies. It is the only way that I can keep the planet alive."

That evening Hunter took Anna to the village where she was able to for the first time see freedom. There were children playing out in the blue sunlight and people walked smiling from structure to structure. There

Hell Found Me

was no sense of fear, no one sheltered themselves from the outside, and everyone looked healthy, and happy.

"Thank You Hunter." Anna said. "You have set me free. I will do all that I can to replenish the planet. If I focus I am sure that I can mend much here."

"Connor will show you what you need to do. As long as you don't go more than a day or two without replenishing what is being taken by the compound."

"I understand." Anna said happily. "I am free. There is nothing I wouldn't do to preserve that."

Hunter smiled as he turned and walked away. Anna felt his contentment, and sighed. She was free and Connor was alive. There was nothing else she needed or wanted out of life.

The leader of the camp smiled as Hunter walked into her chambers. The deal that he made with her all those many years ago that kept her alive and kept him powerful still held strong now, as it was the first day the bond was formed. They would live forever, and they would prosper. As long as she kept Hunter appeased.

"It is done." Hunter smiled to her. "Now appease me woman." He said in a guttural voice as he reached out to grab her, sending wisps of the energy given to him by the people of the 'village' up her leg.

The leader a Neo- Earthling smiled as she let her body absorb the energy he shared with her. Receiving pleasure and giving it back. The bond that they shared allowed her to pleasure him in ways that no woman with physical form could, and allowed her to maintain a physical form.

The inhabitants of the small colony that had mutated to survive on this small asteroid that they at one time thought of as a planet were kept in two groups.

Hell Found Me

The colonists, those that were kept in the settlement for breeding purposes, and the villagers, those that were kept in reactors that filled power cells. The cells that she and Hunter had been selling throughout the galaxy had become one of its main energy sources, they were used for everything from powering ships to providing electricity. There life was long and as long as people lived on this planet the supply would not dry out.

"I would love to know how you get the most powerful of them to do this." She purred from a particularly sensitive spot inside him. Causing his excitement to grow again. "This group was one of the most powerful I've seen in the many millennia that we have been doing this. The 5 of them will power us for many years to come."

"It is quite simple really," The Hunter said. "I give them freedom."

As the Hunter pleasured himself with his bio-mate, Anna Connor and their friends smiled inside the containment fields that they poured their life energy into. Walking through a village that existed in their minds and the Hunter's imagination they fed life to a dream that was in their reality freedom.

TO KILL WHAT YOU LOVE

Hell Found Me

Hunger

Awakening this night was instant and electrifying. The hunger was, as always it's strongest in the first moments of consciousness. It was insistent and all consuming. Many died because its power often caused carelessness.

Fighting hard to control the need Drake watched. He watched and he waited. Shaking off the throbbing hunger he hissed to himself.

"I must be careful. I must not surrender to the hunger."

The chill of rain and the breeze on which it rode whipping into his flesh was a welcome cool, soothing the burning caused by the hunger. The woman would be close enough soon.

She was a waitress in the new club in the 'Party District'. Drake saw her the night before on his way out of the club with his last meal of the night. Upon waking this evening the hunger screamed for her in his mind. Images of her soft pale flesh surrendering to his hunger brought him here. Though the crowded area was not safe to hunt in, the hunger's desire for her held him in the shadowed alleyway.

A woman passed, seeing him huddled in the alley she clutched her purse and walked faster. Reason screamed to him, grab her. Feed now. There is no one to see her disappear. Gain your composure and then go for the waitress. But his need held him in the shadows.

"You control the hunger it does not control you." He told himself.

Hunger

Though it was a cold rainy night his breath had not warmed the air enough to cause a mist to rise from his words. He had not regained the appearance of humanity and it was already three hours after his awakening.

Finally the waitress stepped from the entrance of the club. She was an exotic beauty. Her skin was almost as pale as his was, but it looked healthy. She was of average height with raven hair that flowed around her in the evening winds.

Drake watched as she approached the alley. She walked directly toward him. He stood transfixed by the sight of her. She seemed to flow toward him, gliding on the air more than walking. Her features were strong and the tilt of her chin told him she was accustomed to giving commands.

She was going to get her lunch. His last meal of the night before told him she left the club every night at this time for lunch and did not return for an hour or so. Drake watched her hypnotized. He would not kill her he would enslave her. She would belong to him.

When she reached the alley she stopped just beyond the shadows.

"You should follow me." She said softly. "This place is not safe for the business we must attend to."

"Come to me." Drake said hungrily. He had not stopped to wonder how she knew he was watching or waiting for her. Nor did he question the fact that she seemed to know what would happen, and yet was not afraid. "Come to me. Now!"

The hunger was on the verge of overcoming him. She was within his reach but still in plain sight of the club. Drake reached out and grabbed her wrist pulling her into the shadows of the alley with him.

Hell Found Me

Hunger

She did not struggle as he pulled her deeper into the shadows. She walked calmly and did not protest when he ripped her coat from her shoulders. Turning her back to him and pulling her against his chest he pulled her head to the side exposing her neck and began to feed.

When his fangs sank into her skin she screamed. Her illusions of safety disappeared with the touch of his fangs but it was too late.

"No!" She screamed. "You must not!"

But it was too late. The hunger had overtaken him and his need had overpowered all reason or fear. He would have to think later for now there was only action and reaction.

Then her blood flowed to the surface and the first drop touched his tongue. It was like a red-hot lightening rod had touched him. Power flowed on her blood like none other he had ever tasted. Pulling her closer he hungrily drank deeper. Her blood electrified his body. He could feel it flowing through him making him more alive than he had ever been even before his birth into vampirism.

"Please do not." She sobbed. All of the arrogance and confidence she displayed before he had bitten her were gone. "You know not what you do."

Now that he had fed he had the presence of mind to try to calm her mind as he finished feeding. All thoughts of enslaving her had gone. His hunger had given way to greed. The power he felt himself gaining from her blood made him want more. He would drain her completely. He would have all of the power she carried.

No, I must control the hunger. He told himself. Raising his head from her neck gradually pulling away from the woman he made a new decision. He would keep her and feed off of her every day. Taking small amounts of blood would not kill her and he would have this power source for years to come. When the time came that she no longer filled this need he would kill her. Drake was sure that in time he would be able to find another like her. There had to be more humans like her. He would just have to take the time to find another.

Holding her at arm length he spoke soothingly.

"You need not be afraid. I will not kill you." He said

"You fool!" she said pulling from his grasp. "How dare you feed from me! You will not last the night."

"You are mistaken little one." He said as she turned to face him. "You are the one that may not last the night. The power that rides on your blood does tempt me to take your life. If you continue to annoy me you will die."

Why is she not afraid? Drake wondered. Then it came to him. She must belong to another. She had a master somewhere that feed from her regularly. He or she would be upset with his unwelcome feeding. Her blood was powerful and therefore valuable. She seemed to know her worth, to her master.

"Your master may value your life I on the other hand do not." Drake told her. "To whom do you belong?"

"You are a fool." She said softly. "But I will not hold you completely responsible in this instance. I called you to me last night as you were leaving the club. I did not take the time to search you." She shook her head. "Any vampire with common sense would stay away from me though. How young are you?"

Hell Found Me

Hunger

The conversation had taken a strange turn and Drake was uncomfortable with her comfort with him and the current situation. From her reactions you would think he were the one in danger. He knew that not to be the case.

Looking closely at the woman before him he saw that she was more different from other women he had known in more ways than her calm when faced with an angry vampire. For the first time he looked at her with more than hunger and greed. Looked to her neck, where he could not see the beating of her pulse. Looked to her chest where there was no rise and fall of breath.

"What are you?" Drake asked. Nervous now that his mind had started asking the questions it should have from the beginning of the evening.

"You are young aren't you?" she said. "I am sorry. The truce says I am not to hunt your kind and I will not be hunted. But because I am the last of my kind in this country, and one of only four, no one will question your death."

"My death?" Drake said stunned. "You must be mistaken." He was beginning to become afraid now and he felt the situation had gotten well out of his control. "I doubt you have the power to kill me, especially now that I have fed."

"I am the Night Feeder. I called you to me. If I could control you through the hunger as easily as I have what makes you think you could stand against me in my own hunger?" she shook her head as she took a step closer to him. "You really are weak. Before I feed I would like to know who was your master? Who gave you life? I must know so that your ignorance of me can be punished."

Hell Found Me

Drake was on the verge of panic. Looking into her eyes from inches away his vampire vision told him she wore colored contact lenses. The color of the eyes beneath was red.

"No matter, I will find out Drake." She said. "Your youth makes you easy enough to trace." Then she smiled and he saw her fangs. "Did you know that there once were two families of vampire? One that could exist in sunlight and one that could not." She took another step toward him. "Because one could live in the light the other became jealous and war began. The ability to walk under the sun is a great power in our world."

She held out her hand, and though somewhere deep inside a voice called to him not to take her hand, Drake passively took her hand and followed where she led.

"I will tell you the story of the war between our families." Her voice called soothingly to him through the haze in his mind. "So you will not die in ignorance."

Drake listened as she told him of the two sisters who were born vampires, the story of their children and their treachery, the story of a war that almost removed vampire-kind from the earth. She soothed him with her story of history as she slowly took his unnatural life from his body. As she took the last of his life she whispered softly into his ear.

"And now you die, but not in ignorance. I am Mother Succubus. Mother of the first family of vampire."

The cold darkness of death closed over him like sleep over a child.

And now presenting... Their Father

They had him, the bastard, they had him by the balls and they knew it. How dare he think that they like the other weaklings on his land could be cowed by threats and a little violence? Life was violence life was pain and as the leader of the group looked at the boy that was their ticket out of serfdom and into stone walls he knew, life was blood.

They stayed on the move from the moment that the boy was taken. It amazed their leader how easy it was to walk onto the master's private land and take his son. An easy task made all the more simple by the fact that the boy had not screamed for help when the large wolf loped across the yard toward him. The child had in fact only stood looking at the animal in confusion.

This was the third day that they had the boy and though they were not planning on killing him too soon they did want the master of the house to know that they meant business when they said that they were not playing games. On a daily basis they would hold the child down and shave a strip of skin from his back to send to his father. It was the poor luck of the child that they were hungry and that the taste of blood was a treat. No one bothered to listen to the screams when they licked the child's wounds until the bleeding stopped. So what if there were some that may have nibbled the cuts around the edges to make sure that it bled as long as possible the child was to die within two weeks anyway.

Hours had passed since they'd made camp the leader glanced at the child sleeping in a small lump as close to the fire as it could get huddled in on itself to be as small and unnoticed as possible. The child's simple but well made clothes were dirty rags and it coughed in his sleep.

A howl pierced the night long and wailing filled with sorrow and fear. The sound brought all members of the camp to attention. They did not recognize that voice and though it was in the distance it was a trespasser and could be a threat.

"Go" the leader growled to his two strongest "find whoever it is and take care of them. We are still on our homeland there should be no unknown here."

The howl awakened the child who shivering sat up looking around afraid, but…

A hard kick to the stomach of the child had it coughing blood and cringing away from the members of the pack.

The sound of a howl cut short by a dieing scream pulled the leader's attention from the child. The howl that he had heard earlier pierced the night once again, but this time it was impossibly closer, no one could have traveled that distance in such a short time. Who was this intruder?

"You…you… and you shift and form an outer perimeter, take those three with you" the leader instructed pointing to the chosen guards. Just as the group turned in the direction that the howl had come from a small woman of what looked to be about eighteen years stepped into the clearing, she was dirty and barefoot, she looked as if she had not slept in days. Her eyes darted across the campsite and settled on the boy.

"Who are you" the leader growled the threat in his voice clear.

Hell Found Me

"Okasan" the child whispered trying to stand body shivering and raked by a bloody cough.

"Little bastard" the leader of the group hissed striking the boy on the head the boy's small body fell to the ground. The sound of pain mixed with rage forced its way from the woman's throat past her clinched lips.

"Master Come to Me," the woman whispered a moment later.

As if the darkness itself formed him the child's father stepped into the clearing. The Master's skin unlike the boy's was not pale but his features were the adult version of the child's innocent beauty. Standing beside the small woman the boy's father looked like a giant, his dark hair formed of shadow grey eyes that shone silver in the moonlight darted around the campsite and settled on the child a motionless lump beside the fire.

Worry lines creased the face of man that the leader could no longer think of as master his clothes were caked with dirt, and the leader of the group smiled when he saw the trails of dried tears streaked down the once arrogant and emotionless face.

"How the mighty fall." The leader of the group smiled leaning over to lift the body of the child.

"Okasan my son he is…" the deep rumbling voice chocked on the question.

"No master he is alive, but hurt badly." The woman said "I can hear his heartbeat."

The boy's father, the master and king of the land on which they stood took a deep breath, exhaling he looked as if the weight of three worlds had lifted from his shoulders.

"Then all is not lost." The voice was once again arrogant, and though the clothes were still dirty and the face still streaked with tears it was as though all the grime was washed away.

"Is that so Master?" The leader asked condescendingly. Nodding to the ten men that stood behind him the leader gave the signal for them to shift form two at a time so that they would only be two men down were the enemy to attach mid change.

"You come here with only two people, a girl and a father half out of his mind with worry to face us. You will die, then we will take pleasure from your son and take over you home you money and your land, oh and then your other son will become our slave for a time as this one was."

"Okasan take the boy home, I will deal with this alone."

"But master I don't want to leave" the woman said eyes glued to the child as they had been from the moment she arrived.

"Okasan take my son home he needs attention, I smell his blood all over them."

"Drakhvar..."

"They hurt my son." The boy's father hissed rage and pain flowing from his lips like pieces of his broken heart into the night air.

Nodding the woman took a deep breath and throwing her head back howled into the night long and loud a howl filled with fury. When she looked at the group again her eyes were blood red but there was no other change in her. "I will have him home in less than three hours," the woman said.

Before she could take a step to walk across the clearing to get the boy the master laid his hand on her shoulder staying her movement.

Hell Found Me

Looking deeply into the eyes of the leader of the group the Master said, "No, let him that thought to take my son bring him over."

The leader of the group was desperate to stay away from the silver eyes that commanded him to bring the boy over, but he could not stop himself. Soon he was placing the boy gently in the arms of the woman who snapped at him like an angry dog before turning and disappeared into the night.

"Sit here by my side" The Master commanded and the helpless leader of the group sat. For hours the former leader of the small group watched as the vampire ripped limbs from and disemboweled his closest friends. The vampire bathed in the blood of his friends and family saving the leader for last. When all others were dead the leader was compelled to dig a deep hole in the ground, the vampire crawled in taking the leader with him and covered them with the loose earth.

Oh... I'll introduce you, this is The Oldest Brother

He was sure that he would enjoy his time in Prague there was a supplier in that region with which he'd been having an affair that spanned tens of decades. There was nothing like spending time with a person whose flesh you'd spent decades mapping. She was small durable and forever young. Beauty, something that he held little value for in the modern sense of the word was something that most would say she did not possess, power however she had in abundance.

"It is good to see you," she purred as he entered her room through the open terrace door.

She knew that he would be arriving that night and she also knew that her room would be his first stop, there were few in their community that did not know his family and though most thought of his two youngest brothers as the horrors of the (three) she knew the fact, he was the most frightening of that batch of monsters.

The start of their affair had been in the midst of a battlefield, one in which he stood in the center atop a mound of his conquests, mangled bodies his castle blood filled his moat. There were times that she thought of that night and shivered within her soul.

"You were thinking of the first time you saw me just now," He smiled evil and crooked and she knew that this would be another encounter that she would barely survive. Her heart fought to escape, it knew what he would do... she could not help but to tremble, not in anticipation, or anything as mild as fear.

"I hear your blood trying to escape me, and I feel your desire for..." The whimper that escaped her pleased him, she knew because he sighed as he approached. "You do know that you please me don't you, that it would displease me greatly if you were to die."

For a fleeting moment a frown shadowed across his beautiful features and she remembered why she loved him. The knowledge that no matter what he would not intentionally kill her was not the reason. Life and death to someone that had lived as long as they was of less importance than the knowledge that her demise would pain him in some way pleased her in a way that physical safety could not. But there was another thought that brought a smile to her lips and a lusty quickening to her heart.

He paused with one foot on her bed and looked into her eyes "I please you" He sated calmly removing his shirt and unbuttoning his pants.

"You do" She said letting her confusion show.

"I terrify you" He whispered standing on her bed to remove his pants

She smiled and grunted in reply gazing up at his now naked form

"I own you," He whispered seductively as he placed his left foot on her throat.

Hell Found Me

Oh… I'll Introduce you, This is The Oldest Brother

"From the moment I saw you" She whispered as the pressure on her neck increased.

His reply was a satisfied grunt, taking a deep breath he said "Now you know the only rule is…"

"Don't die," she said as she gathered power inside her to defend…to fight, with all her might, for her life.

Just as the sun began to peak over the horizon he looked down at her. He smiled as he shuttered the windows and closed the curtains on the huge bed he would spend his day in. Settling into the blood soaked sheets he pulled the broken body of what would in a month or so be identified as the woman he saw the night before into his arms, one of which was useless. She was powerful indeed. If she could have lasted just a few hours longer she would have had him with the coming of the sun.

"Thomas," she whispered as she retreated into unconsciousness

A satisfied grunt was his response as the sun commandeered the sky.

Peter looked into his older brother's eyes as they settled into the back seat of the large car that would transport them to the hotel or rather the run down shack of a motel that their youngest brother was hold up in. Why it was that Peter was the only one aside from the newest addition to their family their mother that felt Sasha's dealings were unacceptable. Peter was still taken aback by the fact that their father had given up on trying to tame Sasha, the last conversation Peter had with his father in regard to his younger brothers had ended with their father shaking his head and asking if the result were truly worth the effort.

"Honestly Peter" Thomas said with a sigh looking into his first brother's eye. "I don't understand why you are so concerned with what they do. The day will come that they will learn their lessons…"

"Or die" Peter said with a shiver.

"Do you think that they would be weak enough to be captured, or stupid enough? Not to mention that no one would dare kill them, unless we were already dead." Thomas asked in a calm voice letting his eyes slide closed as his head lay back against the headrest. "This is nothing to worry about."

Peter looked at his brother and sighed knowing what he had never said could prove to be the most important dialog to pass between them. "It is not about them being weak or being stupid, though Sasha has stupidity enough for the both of them." Peter said in a calm voice. "Sometimes things happen, what if they were taken unaware."

Thomas groaned not opening his eyes, taking a deep breath he responded to the worry he heard in his brother's voice. "I know that you are not weak and you were taken, and that my love was quite a feat, but the one thing that they have that you did not is criminal intent and a criminal mastermind working diligently to not only keep their enemies from capturing them but a dogged older brother. Do you think that it is possible for anyone to take Demetri unaware?"

"It could happen" Peter said, "and I was not taken unaware I was just taken... twice... I am the weak link in the family chain." Peter looked out of the one way reflective glass at the blinking neon sign that buzzed in the cool night air. "Thomas would you promise me something?"

Thomas knew his brother and from the tired tone is his voice Thomas knew that Peter was about to say something that all of the family had been expecting but none of them wanted to hear, Peter his first brother and the one person in the infinite universes that Thomas loved more than he loved himself was about to speak of his own demise.

"When I die, promise me that you will take care of them, just as I have." Peter sounded tired and desperate. "You have to promise me that you won't just let them fall by the wayside, that you will make sure that you know at all times what they are doing or at the very least where they are. I will give you all the information that I have and I will show you how I keep track of them as soon as I can, please Thom this is important to me this is the only thing that I worry about when I die."

"This is what you worry about when you die," Thomas said opening his eyes and leaning forward angrily to look Peter in the eye. "What of me when you die, do you not worry about that? Do you not think of what will become of me without you?"

Oh... I'll Introduce you, This is The Oldest Brother

"No my brother... love" Peter leaned forward and caught Thomas behind his neck leaning in to press their foreheads together and look his brother, his closest friend in the eye. "When I die all that is mine will be yours all the power that I wield will be yours and I know that you my best friend will live safely cautiously, you kill all potential enemies and you are not... you are not..."

"I am not what?" Thomas asked wondering what it was about their younger brothers that kept Peter so wrapped up in their safety.

"You are not a child" Peter said reaching out to open the car door.

Thomas stayed his brother with a light touch to the back of his hand. "They are not children either no matter what you see when you look at them. I know that..."

"You don't know... to see them naked and broken... bloody with their hearts barely beating..."

Thomas reached across Peter and closed the car door "Tell me the root of this obsession."

For the first time in over one hundred years Peter told someone why he so doggedly tracked his two younger brothers.

When he got out of the car Thomas was visibly shaken, he was now sure that the two idiots were alive only by the grace of the young fallible god that walked by his side and that it would take a toll on him just as it had

Hell Found Me

on Peter. So many things that Peter said and did that no one in the family could understand now made perfect sense. Their little brothers could have died naked and afraid in an abandoned shack fed upon by humans.

Thomas shuddered at the lurch he felt in his stomach and the emptiness and ache at the thought of losing them. The strength of his distress at the thought of Sasha's death and the idea that Demetri would no longer exist surprised Thomas. Everyone joked that Sasha and Demetri would meet a tragic end but the reality of it was more than Thomas' composure could bear.

"I feel nauseous." Thomas said as he and Peter stepped up to the door.

"Good now you understand." Peter said.

A moment with the Perfect ~~Son~~ Brother

He knew that his younger brothers were up to something he just couldn't put his finger on what it was. They were going to be the death of each other and the downfall of the family.

Alone in his rooms with no one to see it he could smile to himself. How he loved his little brothers. That damn red haired criminal was a great pain in his ass and the blonde was smarter than any living creature should be. They were always causing trouble and breaking rules but 'that is what little brothers do' their father had laughingly told him one night after an especially trying time.

But...

He pulled his mind back to the present something was happening that night and he had to get to the bottom of it. There was a sick feeling in the pit of his stomach and he could not just let them go on their way this time. Grabbing his black trousers shirt and cloak he went to the window of his room best if no one saw him leaving the house this night. He was sure that the two of them were paying at least five of the servants to keep an eye on him.

Just as he made to leap from his window he remembered to grab his staff. For a moment he thought to leave it behind there would most likely be no need for a focus of such power but at the very least he could use it as a cane to beat them with. He leapt from his window and landed softly on the ground below making sure to duck low. He was just under Okasan's window and if she knew that he was leaving the house their father would know as well.

Quickly making his way across the grounds to the small shack that his younger brothers had claimed as their private laboratory and used the key that he had stolen to the large lock. Entering noiselessly he walked to the chair that he knew the red head sat in while the blonde experimented. Resting his hand palm flat on the seat he focused on traces seat finding and illuminating the traces of the aura of the person that sat in it hours ago.

He hoped that the two of them had gone about their business from the house that night and not some other place. He remembered seeing his brothers stop off in their lab before sneaking out with large bags under their cloaks earlier that night so he was relatively sure they had not lugged whatever it was they carried to several locations. Sighing he relaxed his concentration letting the spark of his power set to track his brothers illuminate their trail momentarily surprised by the color.

Following the trail from the house he mused on its bright blue color wondering why the blonde had sat in the chair that night and not the red head. The red head's aura trails were always green as the blonde's were blue so there was no mistaking whose path he was following. As he slowly followed the trail it began to pulse and slowly bleed red. There was a sharp pain the hand that held his staff that pulsed through to his heart.

He immediately broke into a fast run. When the trail that he followed became a deeper red and the pain in his heart grew he pulled from deep within to move faster. Coming to a stop in the shadows outside a large wooden structure that looked as if it had been empty for years he saw the trail flow into the window.

160

Taking a moment to gather his calm and push down the pain in his chest he pulled himself to his full height and walked to the front of the building. Whatever his two little brothers were doing in there needed to stop instantly.

He did not slow his stride as he came to the door that seemed to be in the best condition of the old structure. Raising his staff as he approached he blew the door from its hinges smirking under the hood of his cloak. He knew that whatever they were doing inside would stop immediately at the destruction of the door. What he saw when he entered the structure ripped the smirk from his lips.

His blonde brother looked to be unconscious on the floor in the corner of the room there was a trail of blood from the center of the room to where the blonde lie. If not for the fact that he could see the blonde's form tremble from the cold he would be sure that his little brother was dead.

In the center of the room the red head was chained to a large stone with what looked to be his own dagger sticking into his chest. There were four men surrounding the red head and from the look of it the three women off to the side of the blonde were using some spell to keep him down.

All seven of the people that he saw upon entrance looked at him in shock all frozen by the site of the tall hooded man that stood where the front of their home once was.

"How dare you?" he growled through clenched teeth. None of his features shone to the people in this house the only thing that they could see was the large staff that he held. The sight of his little brothers naked and broken stole his strength forcing him to lean on his

161

staff like an elderly man. "How dare you!" he hissed choking on nausea caused by the sight.

The women looked at him standing at the front of the house, their control for a moment slipping, the blonde's eyes fluttered open to land on him. Though the blonde could not see the face there was no mistaking the voice. The blonde tried to lift his head "brother" he whispered.

Standing there looking at his little brother naked on the floor in a puddle of his own blood reaching toward him caused an explosion of anger within him that humbled volcanic eruptions.

The red head chained naked to the stone with his own dagger in his chest let his head roll to the side "Brother" The red head whispered coughing up blood.

He struck the ground once with his staff his power pulsing through the house that would not stand much longer.

"Let all who walk the planes living and dead in this house bear witness. By the blood of my blood by the life of my life in this plain and the next by my rage and from my soul Hunger Lust and Death are released in this house." He struck the floor with his staff twice. "It is my rage. It is my lust for blood. It is my hunger that upon all shall feed." He struck the floor three times with his staff "Pestilence Unleashed."

The seven people in the house who at the moment of his entrance were stunned hastened to protect themselves. The three women did not have the power to confront their intruder and keep the young man on the flood unconscious at the same time. The men that were in the process of draining the vampire on the stone had nothing but the talismans that rendered vampires powerless. The man at their door who was obviously unaffected by their power was not a vampire.

The three women moving as one pulled strength and power from the man on the floor and hastily threw up a shield to protect themselves. The man at the door was obviously more powerful than the child on the floor and the young vampire on the stone. But why was he there.

The air in the house thickened and looked to contain a red mist. The blood that had been on the floor and across the red head's chest was absorbed into the mist.

"Who are you?" The one of men called to him as the blood mist surrounded and confined him. "Why are you here?" opening his mouth to speak only gave the mist an open orifice to enter.

'You are human" the women said as one "why do you protect this vampire and his consort?" the shield the women had thrown up kept the mist from touching their skin, barely at bay the mist ate at their defenses like lye.

"Demetri can you move?" he asked the blonde, ignoring the seven dead people that spoke to him.

He watched feeling his heart shatter like brittle bone as his little brother struggled to stand to cover his nudity. Gritting his teeth he turned to the red head whose bloody cough was a constant meal to the bloody mist that surrounded the room.

"It hurts' the red head said weakly trying to remove the knife from his chest.

"Sasha" He said softly. His gaze falling on his brother who sounded and looked so much like the small pale red haired boy that followed his every step what seemed to him like just a year ago.

163

"You" he said taking his first step into the house after seeing the scene inside. "You dare" he could barely speak. choking on his rage he threw back the hood of his cloak exposing the same piercing blue eyes and pale skin his younger brothers were graced with. "You dare harm my brothers? My brothers... you filthy humans would try to kill My Baby Brothers?"

His tirade ended with one more strike of his staff to the floor.

"Death!" he shouted.

The mist engulfed the men killing them in a bloody instant. The women tried to hold off the mist but the blood absorbed from the men's bodies made the mist more powerful than the three women even with the addition of Demetri's power. Within seconds they too were nothing but blood in the mist that flowed back to his staff. They were now additions to the blood mist contained in his staff that little bit more power for the next use.

He pulled the dagger from Sasha's chest and holding his staff over his brother's lips allowed Sasha to feed from a little of the blood of the men that had tried to kill him. Removing his cloak completely he walked to Demetri and wrapped his young brother in his cloak and lifted him from the floor.

No words were spoken as he removed his tunic and shirt and gave them to Sasha and with strength no human would possess he carried both his little brothers home one on each shoulder.

As he tucked his little brothers into bed that night watching as their weakened bodies melted into the mattresses his face finally softened.

"Peter" they whispered as they fell into deep restful sleep.

How he loved these two idiots and he had almost...

No one not even the two men Peter tucked into bed knew the fear Peter experienced that night. With trembling hands Peter walked to his window and placed his staff beside it. He would not let them out of his site, ever, he would guard and censor them until he died, or they might.

Introduction to a Criminal

The first time she saw him she knew he must be evil purity could never be so seductively beautiful.

The way he walked in so innocently and yet so sure, he was evil and she must stay away from him at all costs, surely her life depended on it. His hair was the color of fire, his eyes the color of the night sky. Though she knew she should not look in his direction she could not turn away. Her mind fought desperately with her eyes and her body, but the attraction was too strong.

Knowing eyes laughed at her sudden intense blush when full lips quirked in her direction.

Don't call his attention, she thought, if his midnight eyes fix on me I will die.

His body flowed in her direction thick red lashes shielding the hint of his purpose. She knew he must be evil from the pull in her stomach that forced her to stay though she desperately wanted to run when he approached. Nothing good moved so smoothly, so purposefully.

He looked at her across the room, through the crowd. Though in the back of her mind she knew that everyone in the room had not disappeared and the music had not stopped her senses told her that they had. She was the center of the world when night colored eyes focused on her, holding her to the spot where he would meet her, seduce her, and steal her soul.

As he walked across the room she thought desperately, look away! Save yourself!

She could not.

Turn your back on him. He is evil.

She took a step closer.

Midnight became the turbulent ocean as she looked into his eyes. No more than two steps away from him she thought to flee, to break evil's spell on her and leave that place with her life and her soul. The last of her strength helped her to turn away, his feather light touch on her arm stayed her, robbing her of that strength, her will and she knew her life, and soul.

Her heart beat furiously in her chest as she watched the pale fire haired demon take the last step, closing the gap between life and death.

She looked up at him as he took her hand and kissed it in a form of greeting long abandoned looking into those eyes from inches away the turbulent ocean was wracked by storms. Though she was a powerful swimmer she knew that she was drowning in a room full of people.

He leaned in close, soft full lips inches from her own. His breath was warm and misty. He blew softly causing ripples to course through her body. In that instant even the room disappeared leaving only fire, sea and the knowledge that soon all would end. She had drowned in him and she didn't even know the devil's name.

"I am Sasha." His voice caressed her.

"You are a demon." She whispered shuddering.

"You know me then." He smiled voice light with lust filled laughter.

Taking her hand he led her away, out of the room away from the crowd, away from life.

"Do you want to come with me to a magical place?" He asked in the dark of night as he bent his lips to her neck.

Hell Found Me

"I knew you were evil the first time I saw you."
She whispered.

A rumble of laughter against her pulse greeted the last words she would ever say as darkness closed over her.

From the first time she saw him she knew.

Her first thought.

Her last.

They Have a Baby Brother

The young man was rich had the world at his fingertips and he knew it. The young man's dad was a European noble and the young man had grown up with American indulgences. In many ways his life could not get any better or worse.

Walking into his loft condo the young man looked out over the night sky, he still had a room in his father's house, still considered his father's house his home, but here in this place he was free. This was his own palace a little place bought with his money his allowance.

Allowance he scoffed, it still bothered him that his father's four other sons were allowed free access to the family fortune while he still got only an allowance the bite all the more painful when considering the fact that all four of the other sons had fortunes of their own. There was a hierarchy in the young man's family of which he was not a part. Peter the first son was at the top of the food chain accompanied by Thomas the oldest the two of them second only to father as they called the young man's dad. Behind Peter and Thomas came Demetri and Sasha though they were always together Demetri's sharp mind and clinically precise actions placed him before Sasha in the family hierarchy.

There was something about his dad's older sons that sent shivers down the young man's spine, a sensation the root of which he could never pinpoint, was it fear or excitement anticipation or dread of the thought of their presence. The young man thought of when the older sons came to visit him when he was in college. Sasha lived for indulgence and the young man loved the uncaring opulence in which Sasha basked. When Thomas came to visit the young man was reminded of childhood when he would sit with Thomas, Thomas' presence was calming, chilling in many ways but calming. There was something about Thomas that set the young man at ease in the most unsettling of situations. And of course there was Peter the first son. Peter who looked so much like their father and in so many ways was what the young man thought dad was like when younger and rearing his oldest four sons. Peter who was in so many ways reminded the young man of fire, you could barely survive without it, it is beautiful and powerful a bringer of comfort and beauty, its power though sometimes calm could never be tamed, like fire Peter could burn and consume.

Dangerous the young man shuddered the young man's father and other sons were dangerous something the young man was sure that he was not and would never be.

The thought that his father and the other sons were dangerous gave the young man an odd feeling of separation from family. There was something about the young man's family that made him feel that he was just on the outside. The young man's father and father's older sons all lived in a different world as if they were old and lived by codes and rules that the young man's American upbringing coupled with his relative youth could not easily understand. More important than the fact that they were from a different time was the fact that the young man often felt his dad and the older sons were a pack of predators like wolves or lions maybe tigers, they were beautiful as well as dangerous.

The young man often felt that he survived as long as he had because they were not hungry but when the time came that they were in the mood for a meal if he were in their presence he would go the way of the gazelle that played to close to the pride when they decided that they wanted to eat. The young man did not fear his dad having experienced a watered down version of anger from his dad when the young man was a rebellious teen. The four sons had stood in shock when their father shrugged and told him that if he wanted to live his life in ignorance that was his choice but he would not be allowed access to the family fortune. The young man had scoffed. Thinking of that night brought a pull to the young man's lips that could have been a small smile or a grimace as he remembered the night

"So you have not failed all of your classes you just did not attend any of them and were therefore dropped from all of your classes except the two that you just slept through." Father said in an angry voice, it was a voice that did not scare the young man hadn't from the time that he turned 16 and learned that his father had many much more important things on his mind than punishing an errant child.

"I don't think that I was dropped from all my classes." The young man said in a clam reasoning tone. Looking over his shoulder the young man noted the expectant look on Dad's sons' faces. They all looked like they were expecting something, something harsh from their father, the young man shook his head he was dealing with his dad not their father. "I think that I will travel the world for a while maybe a year or two and then once I have seen what life has to offer I will return to school with a more settled mind, I will know what I want out of life and it will be easier for me to focus."

"So you want to travel, see and experience life? Where has this sudden wander lust come from so soon after Natasha's commencement and announced plan to travel to his family's homelands?" dad asked settling into the chair beside the large one the young man sat in… their father's favorite.

Sasha and Peter's gasps could be heard from across the room where the four others stood beside the fire. Turning his head the young man noted that the shock that Peter and Sasha could not keep quiet was written in bold contrast on all four of their faces.

"What?" the young man asked wondering what they were in awe of.

Sasha known to have the least self control broke the silence. "Father" one scandalized word

"If you do not want to go to school at this time you don't have to, take some time and see the world if you want" his dad spoke calmly rising from his chair.

"Thanks dad" the young man said with a smile standing so his dad could settle into his favorite chair.

Hell Found Me

"But you do know that you will have to use your own money.' His dad said as an afterthought. 'Until you are enrolled in school and performing acceptably you will no longer receive an allowance."

"Ok dad" the young man said shrugging off the threat of withheld funds. The young man was not worried about money, never had though the young man had always received a personal allowance he never spent any of it, his father had special accounts set up to pay for things. The young man had savings to last for years taking a step over to sit in the chair his dad had just vacated the young man was stopped short.

"I have things to discuss with your brothers." Father said in a dismissive voice.

"Dad…" the young man began but noted that the four others had advanced to take places around their father, and as such were surrounding the young man though the young man was not worried about his dad denying him anything he could tell from the look in the eyes of the four others that their patience with him was at an end. "I'll go then." The young man sighed sadly, not for the first time feeling the gap between his relationship with his dad and the bond the four others had with their father.

"Do not be sad little one," the young man's dad told him in an appeasing voice, "I will assign you a corporate transport account, but you are responsible for all your expenses"

Hell Found Me

"Thanks dad" the young man said and with an impulse that he was sure the other four would never act on the young man hugged his dad tightly. "I love you dad, and I promise, I'll come home soon and I will study hard, I just want to be... I don't know... I'm just not ready for the responsibility that will come after."

When the young man hugged his dad tightly he closed his eyes so he would not have to see the other four looking at him like a weak stranger coddled by their father. The young man sighed when the embrace came to an end dreading the look of condescension he knew was in the eyes of the other four.

Turning quickly the young man left the room so that his father's sons could have their meeting. From just outside the door the young man heard Sasha his favorite of the other four speak.

"Dad..." Sasha's heavily accented voice questioned.

"Did you see that he sat in Father's chair before father himself could even speak? He scoffed the education requirement. Father is allowing him to travel, with no education. In his last year of university" Demetri said aghast. 'Who are you and where is my father?"

From his spot just outside the door the young man listened to their father's deep commanding voice, a voice that was always tempered when speaking to the youngest, no the young man was not the youngest, Sasha was the youngest, the young man was the baby...

Hell Found Me

They Have a Baby Brother

"You should understand more than anyone Sasha, and Demetri in all your dealings with Sasha can you not understand him at all. He is an infant"

… There his father had just said it; he was the baby the infant of the family.

"He is an infant because you allow him to be." Sasha said in a stern voice. "When I was his age I was an infant as well."

"You were never as innocent as he is" father said in a cool dismissive tone. "You are all older wiser and more powerful than he will ever be, it is your job to understand and protect him at all times and in all things. This is my wish."

The way their father spoke of his wish made it sound more like a command than anything else, the young man did not understand the formal tone of it.

"Then it shall be done" The other four said just as formally.

"… But father I do not understand why you coddle him so. He is not …" Peter stated.

"Finish your thoughts my son" father said in a patient voice. Listening outside the door the young man noted something that he had never noticed in the past. When speaking to the others their father spoke as if to peers, young but respected. Father listened to their opinions and took their advice in matters of business. Peter most of all was a valued confidant, Demetri was

175

Hell Found Me

referenced as if he were an encyclopedia, Thomas was relied upon even Sasha's opinion was taken under consideration, but when father spoke to the young man it was always as to a child.

"We worry that your indulgence is enabling him to be weak and therefore a weakness to the family." Thomas the most understanding of the others said calmly. "It may be that he has a relationship with you that none of us ever had or it may be that because of the time in which he was born there is no choice but to treat him differently, but he is…"

There was a long pause the young man waited holding his breath… finally hearing what the others thought of him

"Demetri, what do you think of this?" Father asked.

"I think that we are all in some ways jealous of the relationship that you have with him." Demetri said in a voice that spoke of someone observing a situation and commenting on it

The young man was shocked by the admission that the other four could be jealous of him for any reason.

'I know that there is a part of me that awes every time I see him embrace you and the ease with which he tells you that he loves you. He is like a normal human child, in a way that none of us ever were. The relationship that you have with him is one that none of us ever could have had with you because he is a person like none of us are." Demetri paused and the young man could hear the smile in his voice. 'The lenience you allow him would never have worked on Sasha. Even with an iron fist and an enforcer wars have resulted"

"What" Sasha tried to protest but stopped short. "Demetri is right, as always, he is innocent in a way that none of us ever were because he is the only one of us that was ever truly human." Sasha sighed. "But father the one thing that you must understand is that you are not doing him a service in being soft on him. And from his reaction to you I think that it is too late."

"'So what would you suggest?" Father asked Sasha.
"You have given him permission to take this leave." Sasha said. "I think that you should turn him over to us as soon as his sabbatical is over."

The young man stood frozen in the hall, terror crept up his spine. Dad wouldn't do that would he? Dad wouldn't turn him over to them, he couldn't.

"I don't know that turning him over to you would be in his best interest." Father said in a dismissive tone, voice wary. "You are already under supervision yourself."

The young man's relief was tangible in the air around him.

"And what when the world learns of him" Sasha asked. 'Were it me he would be my first target."

177

Hell Found Me

"That is untrue" Thomas said 'Not in the direct sense of the word first at least."

"It would be folly for anyone to harm him" Peter said dismissing Sasha's warning. 'He is ours our brother and to harm him is to suffer our wrath."

Something in the protective possessive tone in Peter's voice startled the young man and made him blush… they thought of him as a weak link, that the young man was aware of but the fact that they would feel this strongly about his safety…

"Correct" Demetri nodded, "And to possess him…?""

"Whoever took him would have to be powerful enough to hide and hold him." Peter said, but something in Peter's tone told the young man that he was convinced.

"So how do you propose we do this?" Father asked.

"Let Demetri take control of his education, then when he is out of school have Thomas take over his self-defense once his self defense is done then I will help him with his life skills."

"Life skills" Father's voice held a smirk. 'I don't know that I want you teaching him your particular life skills"

"And you suggest that I sit this one out?" Peter asked

"Need you ask enforcer" Sasha answered with a smirk.

The young man stood in the hall sheer terror too mild to describe his dread the young man was sure that he was standing on his stomach, the young was sure he could endure any of the others supervision the young man was equally sure that he would not survive Peter's rule. Peter was the only person that could keep Sasha and Demetri under some semblance of control. Peter whose wrath gave the staunchest of father's peers pause. The young man was terrified of Peter, the one person the young man was sure that father adored above all others. Peter the one person that the young man knew without a shadow of a doubt could kill him, horribly and his dad would not even ask why.

"We'll see" Father said in a tone that clearly stated that he agreed with what his sons suggested.

Something inside the young man screamed terror as he stood shaking uncontrollably in the hall.

"Avery" the young man heard Peter call his name from within the room. "Join us"

It was a command the young man could not ignore, the young man walked in as their father stood The young man thought to leave the room.

"He is my son" Father said in a voice colder than any Avery had ever heard. "You would all do well to remember that he is innocent and I will protect him."

Shocked Avery looked into his dad's eyes and for the first time he was not afraid of the others, not even Peter.

"What's up guys?" Avery asked, dad smiled showing his elongated canines as Avery settled into dad's and secretly his favorite chair.

Gray Sky

It had been a long while since last Toshin stood in the great hall of his kingdom. Having married a woman that was heir to the throne of her own land Toshin now King of his homeland spent many of the early years of his marriage away from home and a recent dispute in his wife's land once again pulled them away from Toshin's home sooner and longer than expected.

Toshin looked to his right hand where his wife stood tall and beautiful at his side. From the moment Toshin laid eyes on Mae until he was sure the day he died there would never be anything as beautiful to him as her. Letting his eyes stray to Mae's taunt stomach for an instant Toshin marveled at the fact that someone so powerful would bend to his will even behind closed doors. Toshin was awed and humbled by the fact that at that very moment the proud Emperor Mae carried his child.

Toshin knew the instant Mae felt his gaze on her stomach and quickly raised his eyes to look into her liquid gold gaze.

"Love" Toshin said feeling not for the first time that he was drowning in Mae's beauty.

"Eternal" Mae nodded voice smooth.

The two rulers walked through the great hall side by side. Everyone they passed bowed twice once to each monarch in respect for the ruler of a self sustained land. For what had seemed to Toshin like a lifetime but in fact was a mere forty years Toshin had walked a step behind his wife on her left.

Because Mae was the only child born to parents all thought beyond the age of childbirth Mae took her seat as ruler of her lands well before Toshin who was the oldest son of a King still in his prime.

"Emperor Mae" Toshin heard one of the visiting rulers a lesser king whisper as they passed. The envy and awe in the woman's voice threatened to pull a smile to Toshin's lips.

My wife, Toshin looked to Mae again, finding it harder and harder to keep his eyes away from her making the long marble hall all the longer in his distraction.

Toshin noticed that Mae's eyes were more brilliant than the melted gold used to form the patterns in the stone of the walls. The light of the setting sun reflected off Mae's copper hair highlighting the hints of yellow and red gold found in the long curling strands. Toshin felt his breath catch as Mae turned with a smile to a friend and her scent found his nose. He was again caught in her spell as he saw her golden metallic skin sparkle in the light of the torches.

God how He loved his wife

Finally Toshin and Mae were seated at his, the ruling family's table. Mae as a ruler of her stature deserved sat at his right, unlike so many of the others Mae and Toshin were equal.

It was rare for two rulers equal in stature to wed. Mae and Toshin were the first of the great rulers to do so. It was a long standing custom for rulers who of course were bred warriors to wed healers. It was believed that those who took life should marry those that preserved life to balance the couple. Mae and Toshin still considered young had only been married for 60 years and they found that their love and personalities balanced each other. There were few married couples that were as happy as they, but most importantly there were no others that were as powerful.

A good friend and close confidant of Toshin's once told him that the reason many rulers and especially those with kingdoms as powerful as Toshin's and Mae's did not marry was because pride forbade it. Toshin smiled at the deep throaty sound of Mae's laughter which seemed to wrap the table in chocolate velvet. Not really hearing the conversation he was currently part of between his father and younger brother Toshin decided that Mae was indeed the personification of velvet chocolate. In matters of velvet chocolate Toshin saw no room for pride.

Toshin forced his mind back to the conversation… instinctually he knew that they were speaking of Mae.

"…It is indeed rare that a woman hold so completely an empire of such size and power." One of Toshin's father's ministers was saying. "Though the two kingdoms are separated by the wastelands and two minor monarchies they are indeed powerful."

"Well as the only living child of the past ruler" Toshin's mother king of a minor kingdom said from her seat to his father's left slightly behind as her lesser stature demanded. "If there had been someone… a younger brother… to challenge her right to rule then…"

"She would have annihilated them" Genji, Toshin's youngest brother said. "I have seen none so powerful as the Great Emperor Mae."

Toshin fought down his growling laugh, his youngest brother's admiration of his wife was cute and Toshin had appreciated having at least one close family member that supported the union in the early years.

Hell Found Me

However the older Genji got the more Toshin noticed lustful glances.

"Well I will admit she is strong" Naoe, Toshin's second brother said in the most condescending of tones. "And she may have won a challenge to her throne, but those golden skinned savages" Naoe nodded to Toshin "Though extremely beautiful, are savages none the less."

This was an infected thorn in Toshin's side. His family namely his second brother Naoe for some reason resented Toshin's marriage to Mae. Toshin did not understand why Naoe had an issue with his marriage aside from the fact that when Toshin had first married Mae he spent most of his time away from home. There was nothing in their marriage that detracted from Toshin's love for his family and his lands."

"If you think that Toshin is not fit to rule" Genji said idly running his finger around the rim of his goblet. "Then you need to go back to your rooms go to the back of your closets find the chest where mother stored away your childhood memories find you balls. Glue them on then come back her and claim your right to rule through challenge." Genji said with a snort. "Otherwise shut the hell up no one wants to hear this childish crap again. I think you're just jealous because not only are you not the king but you were not able to even make Mae's notice after she saw Toshin."

"Yakamashii teme" Naoe said quickly reverting to their native tongue so that none of the dignitaries would understand.

"Urusai" Toshin's father said in a low firm voice.

"Gomen nasai Oto San" All three brothers said with a quick nodding bow.

"Better" Toshin's father said looking to his wife who nodded encouraging, Toshin thought, her husband to continue.

"I have to say something" Naoe said glancing up at his mother's nod as if the go ahead were for him and not his father. "I" Naoe paused for a moment standing and clearing his voice.

Toshin looked to his younger brother less than one full year younger than Toshin himself. Toshin could see so many similarities in himself and Naoe. Naoe was equal in height to his 6'6" brother with the same dark blue eyes and silver veined dusky skin. Naoe's skin as Toshin's was thin and the silver of their veins was easily seen a stark contrast to their skin tone. Naoe could have been in Toshin's seat but for one thing, he was born ten months later.

Their culture dictated that the oldest child inherited automatically be the child a girl or boy. A first daughter would be king or emperor and her chosen husband would be the secondary ruler queen or empress. Only the bloodline of the land could inherit the seat of power.

When Toshin first married Mae and she inherited her empire he would have been considered her empress, until coming into his own, but as heir apparent of a self sustaining monarchy just as powerful as Mae's Toshin chose to pass on the title. His family did not want Toshin associated with a secondary seat, though in reality he was Mae's empress as she was his queen. Marriage had no effect on the position of primary and secondary ruler.

The law also stated that the order of birth was not the indication that that child should rule or inherit over others. The right to challenge was a birth right of all siblings and in the event there were no siblings first cousins and immediate family had the right.

Toshin knew from the erect stance that Naoe took and the set of his jaw that Naoe was going to claim his right to rule that Naoe was about to challenge Toshin to single combat for his birthright.

Toshin had never been more proud of his little brother in his life. Toshin could not keep the smile of pride from his lips even when Genji gasped realizing the same thing that Toshin did.

Genji saw Naoe claiming his right as a betrayal, Genji felt that as brothers they should support each other at all times and in the event one of the brothers was in the wrong then they should settle it as brothers behind closed doors. Toshin on the other hand felt that the right to challenge was one of their most sacred and it was one of the reasons that families and lands remained powerful. Toshin firmly believed that If a second or even a third born was better suited to rule then they should stand up for their people and that a single person's pride should not hurt the land and people that they were sworn to rule and protect.

"I claim my right to rule" Naoe said in a calm voice. "And I also claim all that my brother holds as mine own."

Toshin smiled when he heard the claim to rule opening his mouth to commend his brother and accept the challenge when a deep searing pain in his chest stopped him.

Mae's scream pierced the confusion and Toshin looked to his right to see his wife draw her bane as she stood a look or horror and rage contorting her beautiful features.

Hell Found Me

"Mae" Toshin said but the burn in his chest seemed to expand.

"How dare you" Toshin heard Genji scream in rage.

Looking across the table and to the left Toshin saw his baby brother still so young still so frail pull out his battle ax and jump in what to Toshin seemed like slow motion across the table toward Toshin.

Toshin looked down at his chest for the first time when Mae's arm wrapped around him suddenly supporting all of his weight.

I also claim all that my brother holds as mine own.

Toshin could hear Mae crying, the sound of her sobs and the smell of her tears pulled Toshin back into himself. Time began to move normally again.

The burn in Toshin's chest receded to the fury in his heart at the sound of his love being attacked at his home by his family. Reaching deep within Toshin pulled away from Mae and drew his own bane.

"I will kill you all!" Toshin bellowed. Then looking at Naoe Toshin smiled. "I accept your right to challenge. But know this little brother you will never claim what is mine, you have not the strength." Toshin kept his brothers gaze as he pulled the short sword from his chest and tossed it aside. "Come little brother I was ready before your birth."

Naoe smirked and stepped back as armed guards flooded the dining hall. Guests remained seated or moved aside not wanting to interfere in a right to rule claim, or a clash between two kingdoms so powerful. If Toshin were to win his and Mae's kingdoms could destroy or greatly weaken even the strongest of them. If Toshin were to die, which seemed to be the case judging from the sever wound he seemed as yet unaware of Naoe would hold his throne as a grudge. Not to mention the fact that Emperor Mae would bring war not only to Naoe but all who stood beside him.

Toshin fought beside his baby brother and at catching a fleeting glimpse of Genji Toshin was for the second time that night oh so proud of his family... his little brothers. Toshin grunted as he watched Genji hack a bloody swath through Naoe's personal guard. But as the numbers against them increased and the prospect of survival for his wife and his yet unborn child began to wane Toshin began to despair.

Mae seemed to be everywhere fighting ruthlessly killing everything that got past Toshin's defenses as his movements became sluggish from blood loss at the same time herding him this way and that. The feel of Mae's blood in Toshin's cuts as she wrapped an arm around Toshin to steady him stung more than his many cuts or the gaping hole that had miraculously missed his heart when men closed in on them.

"Get him out of here" Toshin heard Genji's voice from miles away. "I will hold them here it is a defendable position the way is too narrow for more than three to attack at once."

"Your death would hurt him" Mae said in a strained voice.

"But yours would kill him." Genji said. "I am sure that my guard will arrive soon. We are in mine own home." Toshin could hear the rage bubbling in Genji how dare they not be safe in their own home.

"You will not die here" Toshin said to Genji taking his weight from Mae. "I will not allow it."

"You have to survive to have the right to boss me around" Genji said bracing himself when he heard

Hell Found Me

the reinforcements for the group that had followed them through the hall to the family wing. "Leave here and protect what I love." Genji smiled as his battle axe sliced through the air. "Mae was meant for me anyway, if she had married me none of this would have happened."

Reaching around Genji's waist in a move much like an embrace Mae skewered the solder behind the one dieing on Genji's battle axe giving him time to dislodge his weapon.

"See how well we work together" Genji said widening his stance and shouldering Mae more directly behind him. "Now go save my lucky bastard of a brother and preserve your beautiful face."

"Go to my home" Mae said wrapping an arm around Toshin. "Promise me that in ten minutes you will leave off fighting and go to my castle. You will wait for me there."

"Mae…" Genji said not looking back as the pile of bodies in front of him grew blocking his movements as well as the solders that tried to attack him.

"Promise" Mae said.

"Promise me little one" Toshin said pulling Mae behind him and toward the secret exit.

"I will if I can" Genji said.

Toshin hated to turn his back and leave his baby brother all the more because of the treachery of Naoe, but feeling Mae at his side Toshin steeled himself against the fate of his brother and focused on the survival of his small but growing family.

Through the passages that were the familial escape tunnel they ran in the darkness coming quickly to the exit in the woods behind the castle Toshin and Mae pushed open the heavy door and plunged into the clearing to the light of the setting sun.

Hell Found Me

Gray Sky

Just beyond the exit with their backs to the sun stood Naoe and at least fifty of his men.

"I have been waiting for you" Naoe said with a smirk. "It is time I claim what belongs to me."

Blood everywhere... love is covered in blood and there is no light. The sound of pursuit rings heavy in the ear and... blood everywhere, love's blood seeping from multiple wounds into the cold ground demands attention and stills all other thought.

Breathe, breathe deeply this is a time that the mind should be... has to be calm, eyes close for a moment hearing focuses internally, on heartbeat, not serene, but in time no longer erratic, closer to calm, it will have to do for the moment. Another deep breath and a sigh, slowly eyes open... to blood everywhere calm shatters like delicate crystal.

A debilitating cramp in the stomach caused by the sound of the frenzied barking of the jackals that peruse nearing momentarily stutters movement. With a last bit of desperate strength love is lifted onto tired shoulders. The screams of pain from an arm that is broken in several places is ignored limbs that want to drop uselessly to the ground are forced to steady love's limp form onto a slender shoulder as legs that want to give out under the pressure of life start to move.

Slowly like lead being melted the mind gives way and the body begins to flow into the task.

Run, closer to the ground faster, longer smoother strides. Run liquid flowing over the ground no more pain water doesn't break it flows over and around obstacles coming apart and then back together. Run love is no

Hell Found Me

longer a weight to bear, love is now a leaf in a stream, Run smooth and fluid, Run.

No longer can the jackals that pursue be heard, nothing can outrun water not even wind can overtake it. Breathing deeply the smell of blood no longer invading the lung thrills through the body spurring on a burst of speed

Run and soon free.

What are we to do a flutter of though that tries to break the surface of the river running wild became running, no thought of direction no time to stop. Run the only clear concise thought. Run the only thing that would see them both through this time.

After what seemed like moments but would have had to be longer senses return. The sun stealing some of the strength of the river calls to front the fact that borders have been crossed. Now in the Inner Land a place that not even those without grasp of reality or borders try to come, and those that have tried never return.

There is danger here reaches the forefront becoming an unknown that slows the run and brings to mind the pains. Slowing but never stopping inventory of love's condition is taken. Love is still alive. Love breathes and love is no longer bleeding, but love is very weak. The once mighty is now low. It will take at least three months for love to heal. Where would love be safe for that time?

Running still through the day and into the night a wall comes into view tall and wood, nothing like the walls in their home that are stone. Maybe there will be a place where love can be hidden. A place that love can be stashed until the mate is healed and can protect what it loves. Running faster into the night forcing the body to bend to will the wall is climbed with the dead weight of love on a wounded shoulder. The inhabitants of this place must be powerful indeed to be in such a vulnerable position with nothing and no one else around to call for assistance.

Once inside the wall the mate notices that the wall circled a large piece of land. In the distance a structure could barely be seen. There is a large pond and a small wooded area. This looks like the type of place love would retreat to when time alone s needed. Sighing deeply, putting one foot in front of the other love is placed on the bank of the pond.

Now the reality of the situation sets in and tears can no longer be held back, there is no more control no more strength. Slowly loves wounds are cleaned blood is washed away and deep wailing cries rend the late night air for hours on end.

Movement in the trees behind is noticed but ignored. There is nothing left. After seeing the wounds clearly it is a certainty love will die, love will die because love went against the parent's wishes and married a warrior instead of a healer. Love is going to die and there is nothing that could be done.

With the knowledge that love will die due to its mate's deficiencies grief becomes unbearable. The scream that tears from the mate's throat is long and raw and full of loss. If love dies… a soft pressure on a mangled shoulder brings blessed darkness, hopefully, the mate thinks as darkness sweeps in, this is the end. At least I will die before love.